D0925519

THE TRANCEND TIME SAGA
TIMELESS

michelle madow

Copyright © 2012 Dreamscape Publishing

All rights reserved.

This book is a work of fiction. Though some actual towns, cities, and locations may be mentioned, they are used in a fictitious manner and the events and occurrences were invented in the mind and imagination of the author. Any similarities of characters or names used within to any person past, present, or future is coincidental.

All rights reserved. No part of this book may be used or reproduced in any manner whatsoever without written permission from the author. Brief quotations may be embodied in critical articles or reviews.

ISBN: 0615692931
ISBN-13: 978-0615692937

DEDICATION

To the fans, for loving these characters and this series as much as I do. Your enthusiasm and encouragement means so much to me, and I appreciate it more than I can say. I cannot thank you enough for showing me that there are people out there who care about the stories I create. I shared a little piece of myself with you through my writing, and you all enjoyed it, and for that I am incredibly grateful.

ACKNOWLEDGMENTS

Four years ago, I wrote the first chapter of *Remembrance* and handed it in as homework for an Intro to Creative Writing class I was taking in college. It was the first time since elementary school that I had shared my fiction with anyone I knew, and I was absolutely terrified. Thank you to my teacher of that class, Bruce Aufhammer, for surprising me by saying you thought that chapter was "the best piece handed in out of the entire class." I didn't expect such positive feedback, and hearing it brought tears to my eyes. Thank you to my classmates, who convinced me that other people would be interested in Lizzie and Drew's story. I will never forget that moment. Your enthusiasm for that first chapter led me to write this entire series.

Thank you to Twila Papay and Phillip Deaver, for taking me on for an Independent Study in my senior year, even though you had never worked with a young adult fiction writer before. Having more time for independent work that semester helped me grow as a writer, and I appreciate your belief in me.

Without the support of Tiffany Ashmawy, Kaitlin Webster, and Alicia Bhambhani, I might never have finished my first novel, *Remembrance*. The three of you believed in me, and because of that, you made me believe in myself. Even though we live far from each other now, I will always remember that. You are incredible friends, and while we don't see each other as much as we did in college, you remain the closest friends I've ever had. Thank you for your friendship—it means the world to me!

To my mom, Anne, my dad, Richard, my brother, Steven, and my grandparents, Phyllis, Paul, Lois, and Selvin—the support and belief you have shown me since I declared that "I wanted to be an author" in my junior year of college has been amazing. I know it's not a "normal" career goal, and I am infinitely lucky to have a family that is standing by me as I go for my dreams and trek through the tough world of publishing. Not a day goes by when I don't appreciate that. I love you guys!!!

Christine Witthohn, you were the first person in the industry to believe in *Remembrance*, and I will never forget that. I hope you enjoy the conclusion to the series!

Throughout this journey I have met some incredible book bloggers, and without their help spreading the word, this series never would have reached as many people as it has today. Specifically, Giselle from Xpresso Reads, Jennie from My Cute Bookshelf, Michelle from Book Briefs, and Tiffany from For Those About to Read. I wish I had enough room to include every blogger who has reviewed my books! Also, a special shout out to Amanda from Book Love 101 for the incredible trailers she created for *Remembrance* and *Timeless*.

Lastly, to Ahjah Richardson, Barbara Kaylor, David Madow, Donna Knight, Fred LeBaron, Joanna Royer, Keelie Dutka, Lauren Setzer, Marshall Madow, Misty Durkee, Sara Avakian, Sharon Diggans, Taylor Knight, and Yoko Madow—thank you for your support of the Transcend Time Saga!

ALSO BY MICHELLE MADOW

The Transcend Time Saga
Remembrance
Vengeance
Timeless

The Elementals Series
The Prophecy of Shadows
The Blood of the Hydra (coming April 2016)

The Secret Diamond Sisters Trilogy
The Secret Diamond Sisters
Diamonds in the Rough
Diamonds are Forever

CHAPTER 1

"I can't believe you've never made s'more's before," Drew said, jabbing a marshmallow with an iron s'more stick and handing it to me.

"Not all of us went to fancy summer camps when we were younger where we made s'mores and sang Kumbaya around a campfire." I laughed and took the stick from him. Luckily we weren't sitting outside—New Hampshire at the end of November wasn't conducive to that, and I hated the freezing cold. Instead, we sat in front of the fireplace in Drew's living room, surrounded by a bag of marshmallows, a Hershey's chocolate bar, and a box of graham crackers.

The living room was huge, probably as big as half of my house, and being in there felt like being back in time. The furniture was French antique, and the hardwood floor was covered with a woven Turkish rug. I loved curling up my toes and feeling the softness of it underneath them.

With the fire blazing and Drew sitting next to me, I felt happier than I had in years.

"That wasn't all what my summer camp was about," Drew said as he prepared his marshmallow on the stick. "We also played sports, and did color war."

"What's color war?" I asked.

"My camp colors were blue and buff, and at the end of the summer we were assigned to one of the colors as a team," he explained. "We would do cheers and play games against each other."

"I have a hard time picturing you cheering for a color team." I laughed.

"I got into it when I was younger," he said. "You should have seen it. I put zinc on my cheeks and everything."

"You'll have to show me a picture," I told him.

"I will later," he promised.

I looked into his dark brown eyes, the light of the fire reflecting against the flecks of gold inside them. After everything we'd been through in the past few months, it was hard to believe we were here now, making s'mores and talking about our lives.

When I first saw Drew, he seemed so familiar to me, but I couldn't place where we'd met. I felt a connection to him, but I was dating Jeremy at the time, so I couldn't act on it. I also couldn't act on it because for the first two months after we met, Drew pretended he wanted nothing to do with me. He dated my best friend,

Chelsea, and avoided interaction with me as much as possible.

I didn't understand what I'd done to offend him so badly, and it hurt to be treated like that. But as much as I told myself that I shouldn't want anything to do with someone who acted that way, I couldn't dislike him. The undeniable connection I felt toward him wouldn't allow it.

Then I started having flashes of memories from a life long past—a life I'd lived in Hampshire, England in 1815. A life I'd shared with Drew.

Or a life I *would* have shared with Drew, if I hadn't suffered an untimely death in a carriage accident, destroying any chance we had to be together in our past lives.

Because I, Lizzie Davenport, an average high school junior at the Beech Tree School in Pembrooke, New Hampshire, have been reincarnated. It's still strange to think about. There are days when I wonder if it's actually possible, that I have memories of a life lived in a time so different from my own.

Then I see Drew and I know the love we share is stronger than just this life—it runs all the way from the past into the present.

Our love wasn't the only thing that still existed from the past—the tragic end I'd suffered back then was trying to happen again as well. But after I narrowly avoided death in the present when I stopped Jeremy from getting us into an awful car accident that would have paralleled the carriage accident in the past, Drew came clean to me about why he'd been determined to avoid me. He thought if he didn't allow us to be together in current day, it would have prevented the past from repeating, and stopped my death from happening again.

His avoiding me didn't work. Seeing Drew for the first time made my memories of the past bubble to the surface, and after a vivid flashback at the Halloween dance, I approached him about what I was seeing. He confirmed that yes, we were together in the past, although he hid his knowledge of my death. At first I was angry he withheld such important information, but now I understand why he did it—knowing that you died young and might die young again is tough to process.

Since I stopped the accident from happening again, we were now safe to be together, without having to worry about my possible death. It was relaxing to be able to enjoy my time with Drew. The two of us could finally be normal teenagers.

Well, as normal as teenagers can be after realizing they were reincarnated to have another chance with their one true love.

I held the stick with my marshmallow over the fire. The marshmallow hovered over the flames, the edges turning light brown. Drew took another approach, shoving his straight in. A few seconds later, he brought it out and blew out the fire surrounding it. The outside was charred crisp.

I had no idea how he could think that tasted good.

"What're you thinking about?" he asked, squishing his blackened marshmallow between the graham crackers. Even though it was burned on the outside, it was gooey and soft on the inside.

"Just about everything that's happened," I said, rotating my marshmallow to evenly distribute the heat. "I still feel terrible about Chelsea. She had no idea about the history between us, and now she hates me ..." A lump formed in my throat, and I swallowed it away. Drew was my soul mate, but Chelsea was my best friend.

At least she was my best friend until Drew and I told her we were together. Now she refused to be in the same room as me. Thinking about how I'd betrayed her made me feel sick. But I couldn't just not be with Drew, the person I'd been reborn to spend this life with. Anyway, Chelsea's reasons for wanting to be with Drew were superficial. All she seemed to care about were his looks, and her fascination with his growing up in New York City. It was like being known throughout school as "Drew's girlfriend" was more important to her than being with him and getting to know him.

What made me feel terrible was that I handled it wrong. I should have been honest with Chelsea about my feelings for Drew from the start.

But I couldn't change the past, so I had to focus on moving forward.

"She'll get over it," Drew assured me, draping his arm around my shoulders. "You just need to give her time."

"Speaking of time," I said, "We need to make sure I'm back home by 10:00. Curfew on school nights and all." I glanced at my watch, squinting at the face of the clock when I saw it said 5:15. The sun had set hours ago. "That's strange," I said.

"What?" Drew asked.

"My watch stopped."

"It probably needs a new battery," he said.

"But I got the battery replaced last month."

"Maybe you got a bad battery."

"Yeah." I shrugged, unable to come up with another reason. "That must be it."

Since my watch wasn't working, I checked the time on my phone. 9:20. Drew and I had thirty minutes together before I had to drive back so I got home before curfew.

"We'll get it fixed after school tomorrow," Drew said. "Okay?"

"Okay," I said, my thoughts returning to where they had been before noticing my watch had stopped. "I keep thinking about Chelsea, though. She's not the kind of person to forget about how we hurt her—even if neither of us did it on purpose. What if she never wants to be friends with me again?"

"If she doesn't want to be friends with you anymore, then she doesn't deserve your friendship," Drew said. "Besides, you have other friends. You were telling me the other day how you wanted to spend more time with Hannah, and you and Keelie are hanging out now, too. Both of them are nicer than Chelsea, anyway."

"You would know," I said. "You dated her."

"Hey." Drew nudged me with his shoulder. "I thought you were over that."

"I am," I said. "And I know you never loved her. I just …"

"Wish I had been honest about everything from the beginning," Drew finished my sentence. "I'll say 'I'm sorry' a million more times if that will make you forgive me."

"I've already forgiven you," I said honestly, looking into his brown eyes with the familiar flecks of gold around the pupils. "I love you too much to not forgive you."

"And I love you, too," Drew said, touching the silver heart bracelet he gave me yesterday. "Always and forever."

Drew helped me make my s'more, although unlike his, I didn't put a bar of chocolate in mine. I'm one of the few people—okay, the only person—I know who doesn't like chocolate, or sweet foods in general. Jeremy thought it made me a freak of nature. I was only tolerating the marshmallow, which was a big ball of sugar, because it was fun to cook in the fireplace.

Drew remembered how I didn't like chocolate in my past life, either, and he thinks it's cute. I'm not sure how not liking chocolate can be cute, but to him it is.

I didn't say anything as I ate my s'more, surprised that I liked it. This was definitely something I missed by going to a church art camp instead of an outdoor sports camp like the one Drew attended. Once finished, I wiped my lips to make sure there wasn't any gooey marshmallow stuck on them.

"I think my mom is dating someone," I said, stabbing a second marshmallow with the s'more stick.

"Is that a weird thing?" Drew ate his burned marshmallow right off the stick. Apparently we were done making them into marshmallow/graham cracker sandwiches, and were now eating them straight. It was less messy that way, and the good part was the marshmallow, anyway.

"Not weird," I said. "She dates sometimes. But it's never anything serious, and she always tells me about the guy she's going out with. I've gotten run-downs on all her past dates. But she's being so secretive about whoever she's seeing now, and I can't help but wonder why."

"You should ask her," Drew said, like it was the simplest solution in the world.

"Yeah." I rotated my s'more stick to cook the other side of the marshmallow. "I will."

Drew reached for the bag of marshmallows to put another one on his stick. Then I heard a strange sound from the chimney—like something was trying to come through. A frantic flapping, followed by a loud squawk that sounded like a bird.

I didn't have time to ask Drew what was going on before a huge black crow slammed into the fire.

I yanked my s'more stick out of the flame and backed up on the rug, with no idea what to do. The bird's feathers caught fire, combusting around its body, its eyes panicked. I wanted to reach in and help it, but I couldn't put my hand in the flames. Plus, the bird had stopped moving. I had a feeling it was past the point where it could be saved.

Then a sickening smell filled the room—burning flesh. I covered my nose with my hand, not wanting to breathe in the aroma of death. I felt like I was going to be sick. I wanted to look away, so I didn't have to see the painful last moments of the poor animal being burned alive, but I couldn't pull away from the grisly scene. All I could see was the crow's hollow eye socket staring at me. Blaming me. Like it was saying, "You're next."

I shook the thought away—it made no sense. Why had I thought something so gruesome?

"Go into the kitchen." Drew's voice entered my panicked thoughts. "I'll take care of this." He grabbed my shoulders and forced me to look away from the dead bird in the fire. But not seeing it didn't erase the smell. Cooked flesh. Burning feathers.

The overwhelming aroma of death trapping me, leaving me no room to escape.

CHAPTER 2

Once in the kitchen, Drew grabbed a trash bag and filled a bucket with sink water, telling me to wait there before bringing both items into the living room. I collapsed into a chair at the table, unable to clear my mind of what the crow looked like as it fell into the flames. I couldn't erase the helpless look in its eyes as it struggled, squirming as it burned alive, its little body becoming still when it stopped fighting.

I got myself a glass of ice water, needing to do something while I waited for Drew to "take care of the problem." I heard the sizzling as he dumped the bucket of water into the fire. A minute later, the back door opened. Drew must be getting rid of the carcass.

I shivered at the thought.

I walked around the island in the kitchen while I finished my water, needing to keep moving. Didn't crows know better than to fly into smoking chimneys? Didn't that go against every basic instinct of survival?

And why was this filling me with dread—like it was the beginning of something terrible? It was an irrational thought, but as much I tried, I couldn't shake it.

Drew came back into the kitchen a few minutes later. "It's taken care of," he said. He dropped the empty bucket on the floor and washed his hands, using more soap than necessary and scrubbing his skin extra hard.

I waited for him to turn off the faucet before speaking. "Have you ever seen anything like that?"

"Never." Drew dried his hands on the towel next to the sink. "It must have been a freak accident. Birds know better than to fly down smoking chimneys. Survival sense, you know?"

"Survival of the fittest," I quoted what I was learning in my Advanced Genetics class. "That's exactly what I was thinking."

"Hey." Drew walked over and wrapped his arms around me, pulling me close. "It'll be okay. It was just an accident."

"I know." I closed my eyes and breathed in the familiar pine scent of Drew's cologne. "I just have a weird feeling about it, that's all."

"What kind of 'weird feeling?'" He ran his fingers through my curls, and I relaxed at his touch. Being close to Drew was already making me feel better.

I pulled back from his embrace and looked into his eyes. "We're safe now, right?" I asked. "After we stopped the accident from repeating itself ... we have a second chance. A real chance. Everything's supposed to be okay now. Isn't it?"

"Yes," Drew said, confident and sure. "We prevented the past from paralleling the present. You're going to be fine. What happened in the fireplace wasn't anything supernatural. It was a freak accident. That's all."

"Okay." I nodded, wanting to believe him. "No more fireplaces for a while though, all right?" I laughed, trying to lighten up, but it didn't change how I felt like there was something bad in the air. Something dark.

I had to be imagining it. Seeing the bird roasting to death was playing with my mind. Once I showered and slept, I would wake up tomorrow and everything would be normal.

"Deal." Drew laughed with me, but then his eyes turned serious. "Do you want me to drive you home tonight? You're still shaking ... maybe you shouldn't be driving."

"Thanks, but I'll be okay." I straightened and placed the empty water glass in the sink. "Besides, I need my car in the morning so I can get to school."

"Speaking of that," Drew said. "Since we're an official couple now, and your house is on my way to school, I was thinking I should pick you up from now on. But only if that's okay with you, of course."

"I would like that," I replied.

"Are you sure?" he asked. "If you think it's too soon for Jeremy and Chelsea to see that, I understand."

"I'm more than sure," I said, stronger now. "I would love for you to drive me to school."

For a moment, all thoughts of the bird burning alive left my mind. Now that Drew and I were together, everything in my life was finally falling into place.

If only my best friend didn't hate me, then everything would be perfect.

CHAPTER 3

Drew walked me to my car, even though it was below freezing outside, and kissed me goodnight. Now that Drew and I were together, I couldn't imagine how I had dated Jeremy for so long. I probably should have broken up with him before I did—okay, I know I should have broken up with him before I did—but it wasn't that easy. I'd known Jeremy forever. Even though he changed when everyone at school realized he was an incredible soccer player, I remembered who he was before. When he was the boy who I played with in the sandbox in elementary school, when he sat with me in every class we had together in middle school, and when he asked me to the Valentine's Day Dance in eighth grade, even though he was nervous to do so.

At one point, I really did love him, even though that love was different from the magical, everlasting love that existed between Drew and me. Jeremy was my first love, and I will never forget that. Having that relationship made me appreciate what I have with Drew even more.

I got into my RAV-4, waving to Drew standing outside the double door entrance to his house. The full moon shined gently against his skin, the tips of his dark hair glowing with the light. He smiled, and I was happy all over again about how everything had worked out—how Drew and I had crossed paths in this life and could be together.

I still found it hard to believe that reincarnation existed, and that magic was real. I'd always believed in an afterlife, but now with the memories that were slowly returning to me with every passing day, I had proof that there was more than just this life—that the soul lived on after the body died.

It was incredible to think about.

The ten-minute drive back to my house was relaxing, since I didn't have to take main roads. I turned my iPod to the playlist Drew made for me a few days ago. I usually listened to whatever was on the radio, but I liked the songs Drew picked for me. They were mostly by alternative rock bands that weren't famous, but were still talented.

As I drove, I barely had to think about the turns. The drive was so ingrained into my memory that I was on autopilot. I could just enjoy the music and get lost in the words and melodies.

At least that's what I normally did. Tonight, I couldn't get the image of the bird burning to death in the fireplace out of my mind. It looked like it was in so much pain in its final moments. I hated that I hadn't been able to do anything other than watch it die.

Then there was that dark, sinister feeling surrounding the incident. It felt wrong. Like a sign, almost.

I decided to play a game with myself—a game of fate. If the bird wasn't a sign, the traffic light around the next turn would be green. If it was a sign, the traffic light would be red.

I made the turn, letting out a breath I hadn't realized I was holding when the green light shined ahead.

The bird wasn't a sign.

Then the light turned to yellow, changing to red before I reached it. No cars were coming from the other way, but I had to stop.

I tapped my fingers against the steering wheel as I waited for the light to return to green. What did this mean? It was green when I first saw it, but then it became red before I could pass.

Was the bird a sign or not?

This was silly. Logically, I knew the color of a traffic light couldn't give me the answer I needed. I was freaking out over nothing. But the night felt darker, the emptiness of the streets putting me on edge. My skin prickled under the sleeves of my jacket, and I turned the heat up, as if the warm air blowing against my cheeks could erase the unease that filled me.

I wanted to get home and go to sleep, so I could wake up and start fresh tomorrow.

The light turned green, and I hurried across the intersection, wanting to get away from it as fast as possible. Glancing at the speedometer, I noticed I was going ten miles per hour faster than the speed limit, and made myself slow down. I hated speeding. It was reckless, and there was no reason to rush home. My mom wasn't strict about my curfew, as long as I was back around the general time we agreed on. She would say it was more important to be a safe driver and get home five minutes late than to rush and be there on time.

Once the traffic light disappeared from the view of my rearview mirror, I realized how ridiculous I had been about that "sign" nonsense, and made myself relax. Fate was bigger than a stupid game I invented on the spot.

Then chills passed through me, and three blobs of black arched through the sky towards my car. I identified them as crows seconds before they reached my windshield. I slammed the brakes, the tires screeching against the pavement, but it didn't help me avoid impact. The birds thumped as they hit the glass.

I closed my eyes, not wanting to see their broken bodies on the hood of my car. I could feel the rising and falling of my chest, and hear the heaviness of my breathing over the music playing in the background. But everything outside was still.

At least I had stopped without hitting anything big, like another car, or a tree.

Realizing it wasn't safe to remain stopped in the middle of the road, I opened my eyes to survey the damage. There were three circles of shattered glass on the windshield where the bodies of the birds had collided with it, cracks coming out of each one like spiderwebs. Luckily, I didn't see their bodies anywhere. They must have deflected off the car from the impact. I was glad, since I couldn't handle seeing more than one dead bird in a single night.

Even though I was five minutes away from my house, I pulled over to the side of the road to collect myself. I made myself breathe steadily, focusing on slowing my heartbeat to a normal pace. I had to calm down.

I wanted to call my mom, or Drew, but I knew what they would tell me—to try to relax, and when I felt better to continue home, being extra careful. There wasn't much else I *could* do.

Once I was calm enough to drive, I continued down the road to my house. I tried not to think about the crows coming toward my windshield, but the three bird-size circles where they had cracked the glass didn't allow the image to leave my mind.

What did this mean? One incident with a crow I could pass off as an accident. But two?

It had to be a sign.

And I doubted it meant good things to come.

CHAPTER 4

Just got home, I texted Drew after pulling into the garage.

He liked me to let him know when I got back if I was driving somewhere myself. He said he worried about me otherwise. It was sweet of him—one of the many things he did that let me know how much he loved me.

Glad to know you got home safe. I'll see you tomorrow morning, he replied.

My fingers hovered over the screen. I didn't want him to worry about the crows—I was all right, and that was what mattered—but it wasn't something I should keep from him.

Something weird happened on the way back—three crows hit my windshield. I'm okay, but my windshield, not so much. I pressed send.

Another incident with crows? His response came quickly.

Yeah, it's weird, I texted back. *But I don't want to think about it too much right now. I just want to go to sleep.*

I understand, he replied. *I'm glad you're okay. We'll take your car in to get fixed sometime this week. I love you.*

I smiled when I read his text. *See you tomorrow,* I sent back to him. *I love you. Always and forever.*

It was good he was driving me to school tomorrow, because while I made it home fine tonight, I didn't want to drive with my windshield the way it was. The glass hadn't broken, but I worried the cracks would become worse and combust while I was driving. It wasn't worth testing my luck, especially since luck wasn't on my side tonight.

My hands shook as I opened the door to the house, and I was glad to be home. Compared to Drew's, my house was tiny, but it was more than enough space for my mom and me. We may not have fancy antique furniture, but the worn hardwood floors and mash up of pieces my mom and I discovered at the local consignment shops were always welcoming.

I found my mom in the kitchen, pouring herself coffee. I assumed it was decaf. She looked perfectly poised, her dark blonde hair sprayed in a shoulder length bob, and she had on the semi-stylish but sensible brown pants suit she wore to work.

I said hi to her, unable to get rid of the jittery feeling coursing through my body.

"Is everything okay?" she asked when she saw me, her eyebrows creasing in concern.

My mom could always tell when something was off with me. It was probably because she was a psychiatrist. It was her job to sense when people needed to talk.

Or maybe it was because she was my mom, and mothers can tell when something is bothering their daughter.

"Three birds hit my windshield when I was driving home tonight," I said, trying to keep my voice steady. "It freaked me out a little, but I'm okay. Just ... shaken."

She placed her coffee down on the counter, her lips forming into a circle of surprise. "They flew right into your windshield?" she asked. "While you were driving?"

"Yeah." I walked to the display of coffees and teas and picked one labeled Sleepytime. "I was freaked out, but there were no other cars on the road when it happened, so I didn't hit anyone. I was just spooked, I guess."

"You're sure you're all right?" she asked.

"Yes," I confirmed. "I'm fine. But I can't say the same for my windshield. Drew's going to take me to get it fixed later this week."

"Well, I'm glad you're okay." She took a sip of her coffee. "Because I wanted to talk with you about something important. If you're not up for it, I understand, but it's something I want to discuss before you go to school tomorrow."

I wanted to go to bed, but now that she mentioned wanting to "discuss something important with me," there was no way I was going to be able to fall asleep without knowing what it was.

I glanced at my watch to see what time it was, only to be reminded again that the battery wasn't working. Yet another thing I needed to get fixed. I checked the time on the microwave instead. 10:20.

I liked to be well-rested for school, which meant getting a full eight hours of sleep, and even if I went to sleep right now I wouldn't be getting that. A couple of weeks ago I sneaked out a few times to spend time with Drew, and I was tired in school for days afterward. While spending time with Drew in secret was exciting, now that we didn't have to hide our relationship, we decided it was best to not sneak out. He didn't want my mom finding out and not liking him for "being a bad influence," and it was getting too cold for midnight rendezvous on the lake, anyway.

"We can talk about it now," I said, suppressing a yawn. I took my cup of tea out from the instant hot and blew in it. It smelled delicious, but I had to wait a few minutes to drink it so I didn't burn my tongue.

"Okay, good," she said, sitting down at the kitchen table.

I joined her, worrying what this was about. Did I get in trouble at school? I couldn't think of anything I could have done, since I wasn't a trouble-maker. Maybe I did poorly on my Advanced Genetics test last week, and Mrs. Sharon called my mom to let her know? I had been distracted recently with the drama between me, Drew, Chelsea, and Jeremy, but school was important to me, so I didn't let my personal problems interfere with my studying. I doubted that was it. So what could it be?

"What's up?" I asked, trying my tea. It was too hot, and it burned going down my throat.

"I don't know how to say this, so I'm just going to put it out there." She cleared her throat and took a sip of coffee. "I'm seeing someone, and it's getting serious."

That wasn't what I was expecting right then, but I wasn't surprised, either. I relaxed at the realization that I wasn't in trouble, and that I wouldn't have to be the one who asked my mom about whoever she's been dating.

"I had a feeling you were seeing someone," I said. "I wanted to ask you about it, but you were being so secretive and I had no idea how to bring it up."

"I'm sorry about that." She laughed. "It's just that you know him, and I didn't want to make things strange for you until I knew it would work out between us. But things have been going great, so I figured it was time you knew."

"So," I said, leaning forward. "Who's the guy?" I took another sip of tea as I waited for her to tell me—it was the perfect temperature now.

"Tyler Givens."

I gasped and choked on my tea. She didn't say anything as she waited for me to stop coughing.

"Tyler Givens ... as in Chelsea's dad?" I clarified once I could breathe again.

"Yes," she confirmed. "Chelsea's dad."

"Wow ..." I took a moment to soak this in. My mom and Chelsea's dad had known each other for a while—they went to high school together—but I had never pictured them *together*. But now that she mentioned it, I saw how it could work. They were both professionals—he a lawyer and she a doctor—and before Chelsea and I got licenses and they had to drop us off at each other's houses, they did get along well.

But being able to chit-chat for ten minutes and seriously dating were completely different.

The biggest problem with my mom dating Mr. Givens was that Chelsea wanted nothing to do with me anymore. If I thought things were awkward with Chelsea now, they were going to get worse once her dad broke this news to her. She would probably twist this into a reason to hate me more.

"I know you and Chelsea are working through some difficulties right now," my mom said. "But Tyler invited us to Thanksgiving dinner this Thursday at his house, and I was hoping you would consider going."

I stared at her with wide eyes. First of all, it was strange that my mom and Mr. Givens were on first name basis. I supposed this should have been obvious since they were "seriously dating," but it was different to hear her refer to him that way out loud. Secondly, Chelsea basically kicked me out of her house when I tried to apologize yesterday. She wasn't going to be happy that her dad invited me and my mom to their Thanksgiving dinner.

"I understand if you don't want to go," my mom said, although I could tell from the hopeful look in her eyes that she wanted me to say otherwise. "So I told him I would ask you before giving a definite yes."

I wanted to say absolutely not, without giving it any more thought, but I knew better than that. My mom knew about what had happened between Chelsea, Drew, and me—how Drew dated Chelsea first, broke up with her for me, and now Drew and I were dating. I told her after getting home from Drew's when he gave me the bracelet last night, and she took it well. (Although I did, of course, leave out the reincarnation stuff).

She made sure I didn't allow anything to happen with Drew until after he broke up with Chelsea, and I told her the truth, that he broke up with her first. She was proud of me for not allowing cheating to happen. She also said it reflected well on Drew's character, because lots of guys in high school cheat on their girlfriends. She can't give me any names, but some girls from Beech Tree are her patients, and they talk with her about their boyfriend problems. It was strange knowing that girls from your school talked with your mom about personal issues, but that's something you have to accept when it's your mom's profession.

The best part about telling my mom everything was that she didn't make me feel like I was in the wrong for dating Drew after he was with Chelsea. She also told me that it made sense Chelsea was upset, but she wouldn't be mad at me forever.

She wouldn't have asked me about Thanksgiving dinner unless it was important to her.

"I guess it's okay," I said, even though I was worried about seeing Chelsea in a situation like that. There would be only four of us in the room, and no escaping conversing with each other.

At least our parents would be around, so she would have to be civil. But when Chelsea got upset, you never knew what she would do. I remembered one time in ninth grade when Joanna Rowland called Chelsea a slut on her blog. Chelsea got mad, so she anonymously contacted Joanna's parents and told them about the blog (where Joanna also discussed sneaking out to go to parties and other things her parents didn't know about). Joanna was grounded for months. That was the end of her social life that year, and all because she upset Chelsea.

I hoped that because Chelsea and I used to be best friends, the worst she would do was not talk to me for a while. But with Chelsea, you never knew.

"Are you sure?" my mom asked. "I understand if you're not up for it yet."

"Yes," I lied. "I'm sure."

"Maybe this will be good for your friendship with Chelsea." My mom smiled. "You two were so close ... and Thanksgiving is the time for forgiveness."

She sure was chipper. I supposed she was happy because she had finally told me about dating Mr. Givens. Correction: Tyler. Ugh. Could my mom have picked anyone more inconvenient to date? I didn't have a problem with Mr. Givens—he was friendly, and a great dad to Chelsea and her older sister Tiffany—but the timing couldn't have been worse.

"Maybe it will be." I forced a smile that I doubted was believable. Then I yawned. "I'm tired, though," I said. "I think I'm going to go to bed."

"All right," my mom said. "Do you want me to drive you to school tomorrow since your windshield needs to be fixed?"

"Drew said he'll pick me up," I told her. "Even before my car got messed up."

"He seems like a good kid," she said. "One of these days I'm going to want to meet him. Dinner or something."

"Sure," I said, even though I had no idea how that would go.

Hey, Mom, I forgot to tell you something. Drew and I are reincarnated. We fell in love in 1815 in England, but then I died at sixteen in a carriage accident. Now that we've been reborn, we have a second chance to be together without death getting in the way. Cool, right?

She would think I needed to become one of her patients.

I made my way upstairs, glad I would be in bed within the next few minutes. Then, as I took the final step to the second floor, a framed picture of me at eight years old in a puffy red dress standing next to a Christmas tree clattered to the ground.

It made me jump, but at least it didn't sound like the glass shattered.

I picked it up, expecting the back of the frame to be broken, but everything was fine. Putting it back onto the nail, I told it to stay. I let go once satisfied it was firmly in place.

Looking at the picture made me smile—my mom got me a huge Playmobile dollhouse that year. The giant box was behind me, waiting to be unwrapped. It was one of the best Christmases ever.

I yawned again, and walked to my room. But before I could close the door, I heard another bang near the stairs.

The picture next to the Christmas one had fallen—this one of me holding my diploma after my eighth grade graduation.

One picture randomly falling off the wall I assumed was an accident. But two?

I hung it back in its place. Just like the other picture, nothing was broken, and it went back up easily. It was as though someone—or some*thing*—had knocked it off the wall on purpose.

Not like that was possible, since I was the only one upstairs.

Another strange, dark feeling traveled through my body. I checked the hallway for I don't know what—a ghost, maybe—but it was clear. I didn't even believe in ghosts, but with what I'd learned recently about reincarnation, anything was possible.

After determining that no one was lurking in any corners, I went back into my bedroom and shut the door. I had no proof, but I had a feeling that something strange was going on.

And it wasn't something good.

CHAPTER 5

Drew and I walked into AP European History together on Monday morning, only to receive death glares from Chelsea when we stepped through the door. I also noticed how dressed up Chelsea was. She normally spent a lot of time getting ready for school, but this was overkill. She had on a black mini-skirt, and even though she had tights and knee-high boots on with it, she must have frozen walking from the junior lot. Then there was her shirt—a lacy spaghetti strap piece that went so low that I thought her cleavage was going to pop out. And she was definitely wearing a push-up bra. As her best friend—*ex* best friend—I could tell these things. Her eyes were done up all smoky, and with her bright red lipgloss, she looked like a vixen.

If she was trying to get Drew's attention, it wasn't going to work, at least not in the way she wanted. But Craig Woods sitting next to her had certainly noticed—

he looked more awake in first period than he had all year.

"Where do you want to sit?" Drew asked me.

I looked around the U-shaped table, trying to decide which seat would make it so I didn't have to see Chelsea during class. Not like that was possible, since the seats were arranged so everyone could see each other to generate better class discussion. Still, some areas were less in her line of sight than others.

"Over there," I said, picking two empty seats in the back corner.

Drew took my hand as we walked to our seats. I could have sworn that Chelsea's red lips curled into a small hiss.

I understood that she was upset—but she really seemed to hate me. Full-blown, one hundred percent hatred.

It made me feel positively awful.

Class went by slowly, especially since I had to concentrate extra hard on averting my eyes from Chelsea's direction. When it was finally over, she left without a glance at Drew or me, adding an extra strut to her walk. I didn't know what she was aiming for, but Drew wasn't going to fall for Chelsea's attempts to get his attention. Ever. Because he was meant to be with me.

But I also saw where she was coming from. She had no idea how deep my connection went with Drew, and why that was worth risking our friendship. If he were any other guy, I would have ignored my feelings for him, even after he broke up with Chelsea and wanted to be with me. I would have told him that since he'd hurt my best friend, nothing could ever happen between us.

Unfortunately, it's not that simple when said guy is your reincarnated soul mate.

I wished Chelsea could understand, but how did you explain that to someone? She didn't believe in fate and true love—she'd told me herself when I went over her house the day after Shannon's party. In her eyes, I was simply a terrible friend. And as much as it hurt to acknowledge, I understood why she felt that way.

Why did this have to be so complicated?

French passed quickly—now that I had my past self's knowledge of the language, I no longer struggled through class. I used to embarrass myself by messing up the pronunciations of the words, but now the biggest challenge was lowering my ability to speak at the level I should be for AP French. I didn't want to let my teacher know I was fluent. That would arise suspicion, which I didn't need.

French was also my first class of the day with Jeremy, and I was glad when he didn't act spiteful like Chelsea. He was civil, saying hi to me when he entered the classroom before making his way to his seat in the back. I still detected hurt and betrayal in his clear blue eyes, but at least he seemed to be moving on, and he didn't seem to hate me.

I was glad when it was lunchtime, but worried about where everyone involved with the disaster last weekend was going to sit. I planned on eating with Drew, and I hoped to eat with Hannah in the commons, and maybe Keelie as well. But Keelie had been best friends with

Shannon and Amber forever, and she ate with them in the cafeteria.

She'd also left Shannon's party when I called and rushed to help me, so I had no idea if that had changed the dynamic between the three of them. Would Shannon view Keelie's helping me as a betrayal? Keelie didn't deserve that, but it seemed like something Shannon might do.

When Drew and I were waiting in the lunch line, I spotted Chelsea sitting with Jeremy, Shannon, Amber, and the rest of the sports crowd in the cafeteria. No surprise there. It was the same place where I sat in the beginning of the year when I was dating Jeremy, although I never felt like I belonged with them. They were only nice to me because I was dating Jeremy—not because they wanted to be friends with me.

I didn't see Keelie sitting with them, and was happy to find her in the commons with Hannah and some of my friends I've known since middle school. She waved me and Drew over when we entered, motioning for us to sit in the empty couch surrounding the low table. The couch was small—there wasn't room for two people unless they squeezed together—which was fine with me.

"After everything that happened, I thought I would sit with you all today," Keelie said after we sat down. "Plus, Chelsea is pissed, and Shannon's her new best friend. I didn't feel like dealing with the two of them being all dramatic through lunch."

"They're that bad?" Drew chuckled and raised an eyebrow.

"You have no idea." Keelie rolled her eyes. "They're secretive, too, acting like they know something nobody else does. It's super weird."

"Shannon's not upset at you for leaving her party when I called?" I asked.

"She'll get over it." Keelie shrugged it off. "This'll blow over in a few weeks, anyway."

This reminded me why I liked hanging out with Keelie: She was down to Earth and didn't worry about situations that were out of her control. Maybe she was right and everything happening *could* be for the best. Yes, I missed Chelsea, but Chelsea was also a possessive best friend. She got mad if I did something with someone else and didn't include her. Now I could get to know Keelie better, and spend more time with Hannah again, too.

I was about to agree that Keelie was right about it blowing over in a few weeks, until I remembered what my mom had told me last night.

"If I tell you something, will you promise to keep it between us?" I asked Keelie. I'd already told Drew about the Thanksgiving dinner situation in the car this morning, and I knew he wouldn't tell everyone about it. I had a gut instinct I could trust Keelie, too—but I wanted her to verify it first.

"Sure," she said. "What's up?"

Before speaking, I made sure no one else in the group was listening to us. They were all talking about a concert they went to Saturday night, and weren't paying attention to what Keelie, Drew, and I were discussing in the corner.

"My mom and Chelsea's dad are dating." I spoke quietly, so no one could overhear. "We're going to Thanksgiving dinner with them Thursday night. It shouldn't be a big deal, but Chelsea's so mad at me that she won't talk to me, and I doubt she'll be 'over it' in less than a week."

"Hm," Keelie said. "That does sound rough. But your parents will be there, so she can't say anything too nasty with them around, right?"

"Right," I agreed, even though you never knew with Chelsea.

"It sounds like you're stuck going, so the best you can do is not worry about it." Keelie shrugged. "Anyway, it'll be winter break soon enough. By the time we get back in January, this will be last year's news."

"If dinner is awful, just remind yourself that you can spend the rest of the weekend with me," Drew said, pressing his leg gently against mine, as if he was reassuring me he was there for me.

"We can go to the mall on Saturday, too," Keelie said. "I'm going to the Caribbean with my family over winter break, and I need a new bathing suit. A strapless one, so my tan's even when I get back."

"So I'm not going to worry about Thursday," I repeated Keelie's advice, as if saying it aloud would make it true.

Unfortunately, it didn't stop me from worrying about all the ways Thanksgiving dinner could go wrong.

CHAPTER 6

Despite a few nasty glares from Chelsea during Trig, the rest of the day went fine. I kept reminding myself about what Keelie had said—how it was getting closer to winter break, and once January started this drama will have blown over.

Hopefully she was right. I hated drama, especially being in the center of it.

At the end of the day, Drew and I walked together to his car. I pulled my jacket tighter around myself as we made our way up the hill, looking forward to next year when we could park in the senior spots in front of the school. The walk to the junior lot wasn't terrible in the fall, but now that winter was coming, it was annoying to deal with the weather. My cheeks were flushed from the cold once we made it to his black BMW.

"Let's go to your house first and get your car so we can bring it to the shop," Drew said, opening the door for me. "You can't be driving around with your windshield smashed up."

"Okay," I agreed, although my mind was somewhere else. I couldn't stop thinking about the bird in the fireplace, and the three crows colliding with the glass when I was driving last night.

It felt important, but what could it *mean*?

Drew shut my door and walked around to get into the driver's seat. Then, out of nowhere, a crow landed on the hood of his car. Right in front of the windshield. It was followed by another, and one more after that.

What was going on? They were acting like the hood of his car was covered in bird food.

I tapped the glass to scare them, but they stayed put, staring at me, threatening me with their dark beady eyes that peered deep inside of my soul.

But that was a ridiculous idea. They were crows ... they didn't *think*.

"What on Earth ..." Drew said as he slid into the driver's seat. He turned the car on, and the engine revved to life. I thought that would scare the birds away, but they remained where they were.

Then they started to peck on the glass.

"Get them off!" I said, pounding my fists on the inside of the windshield. Instead of flying away, they pecked harder. Then three more landed on Drew's side and pecked there as well. It was like something out of a horror movie. They wouldn't stop. It was like they were out to get me.

But how was that possible?

I pressed my hands over my ears, trying to block out the echoing tap-tapping that was ingraining itself into my skull. Their black eyes looked angry now, and they stared at me, pecking harder with each second, like they were trying to get inside.

How much longer could Drew's car take this?

Two more birds flew up to the window next to me, and I couldn't help it—I screamed. They pecked harder now, and cracks spread across the windshield.

Drew peeled out of the parking spot, not checking if any cars were in the way, the tires squealing against the pavement. The moment the car moved, the birds flew away.

"Don't tell me that was a coincidence, too," I said, looking behind me to watch the group of birds fly away, a clump of darkness against the overcast sky. At least they weren't following us.

He shook his head, his lips pressed firmly together. "I wasn't going to."

"Ever since last night, I've had this strange, spooky feeling," I said, taking a few breaths to calm down. My hands wouldn't stop shaking, though. "I feel like something's following me. Something ... evil."

I ran my fingers through my curls, realizing how crazy that sounded. Why would anything evil be after me? I was a good person for the most part. Yes, I'd made mistakes, like not breaking up with Jeremy when I should have and not being honest with Chelsea about my feelings for Drew from the beginning, but I was only human. People messed up sometimes. What mattered was that we learned from our mistakes and didn't allow them to happen again.

It didn't seem fair that I was being punished for a few little mistakes—if that's what was happening. Maybe I was being delusional ... but I doubted it. These strange things that were happening to me had to mean something.

Drew turned right out of school. The way to my house, where we had to go to get my car, was left.

"Where are we going?" I asked.

"The mall," he said. "We're going to Alistair's. Because as much as I wish I had answers about what's going on, I don't, and he might."

With that, we headed towards the mall, Drew's hand not leaving mine for the entire drive.

CHAPTER 7

Alistair's shop was in an offshoot from the main section of the mall, away from the food court and department stores, so you wouldn't know it was there unless you were looking for it.

I remembered the first time I went to Alistair's in October, when I showed him the sketch I'd done of the mask I envisioned wearing to the Halloween dance. He was friendly, and not only did he make the mask for me, but he gave me a great deal on the white dress I ended up wearing to the dance, and a necklace for free. A few weeks later he gave me one of the best presents I've ever received—the original three book printing of *Pride and Prejudice* by Jane Austen. They were on display in my bookshelves now. I'm afraid to read from them, since they're antiques and I don't want to mess them up, so whenever I feel like reading a section of *Pride and Prejudice*, I use the paperback I keep on my nightstand.

I've only had the book for a few months, but it's already well-worn, or as I prefer to think of it, very loved.

At first I wondered why Alistair was being so generous—giving me items for free or reducing the price to far below the original value. After realizing the truth about my past life, he was the first person I visited. I suspected he knew something—I couldn't figure out any other reason why he would have given me those things—and I was right.

It turned out that Alistair is a Memory Guide. He had already been through the reincarnation process—his first life was in medieval England. He was given a second chance by being reincarnated into the Civil War era, and he corrected what he'd messed up the first time around, which was saving his own life in battle instead of risking death to save his brother Tristan, who had been badly wounded. After he died in his second life, he was given a choice: to enter Nirvana, which is similar to Heaven, or to return to Earth one last time as a Memory Guide and help someone who'd been reincarnated remember their past life. He chose the second option, and was assigned to me. That's why I was drawn to his shop, and why he provided me with the items I needed to help me remember the past.

Of course, he couldn't tell me all that until I figured out on my own that I'd been reincarnated.

I suppose that meant after I died in this life, I would have to make a similar choice between Nirvana or becoming a Memory Guide. I planned on choosing Memory Guide. I would love the opportunity to help someone like Alistair did for me.

But hopefully that wouldn't be a decision I would have to make for a long time.

Right now I had something more important to worry about—why bad things were following me everywhere I went, and why I couldn't shake the feeling of doom surrounding me.

I felt at home the moment I entered the shop. It was dark inside, the only light coming from the antique lamps scattered throughout the store. The shop was packed with various trinkets from all over the world. I recognized one I'd admired the first time I visited—a horse pulling a golden carriage with crystals inside. It looked romantic, but after the terrifying flashback I had a few days ago of when I died in a carriage accident in my past life, I had no desire to go in one myself.

"Back so soon?" Alistair asked from behind his big wooden desk. He reached for his cane and stood, motioning for me to walk to him. He wore a tweed suit, which made him look like a wise old professor, and his eyeglasses were tucked into his front pocket. His grey hair shined under the low light, and his eyes had a familiar twinkle to them, like he knew something others didn't.

I grabbed Drew's hand and led him through the maze of tables. "Hi, Alistair," I said once I reached him. I was sure he was wondering why I was here, since my last visit to the store was Saturday afternoon.

I couldn't believe only two days had passed since he sat down with me and told me about his history. It felt like so much had happened since then.

"Who is this with you?" Alistair asked with a knowing smile.

"I'm Drew," Drew said, holding out his hand to shake Alistair's.

"Drew Carmichael?" Alistair asked.

"Yup," Drew replied. "Lizzie's told me a lot about you and how helpful you've been to her in the past few weeks. I'm glad we're finally getting to meet."

"Me too, me too," Alistair said. "Let's not stand, though. Come sit down." He motioned with his cane to a round table, and the three of us each took a seat. Once he got situated, he said, "Now, tell me what's on your minds."

My eyes met Drew's, silently asking who should start. He nodded for me to begin.

"We have a question, and you were the first person we thought to come to for answers," I started. Alistair nodded, and I continued, "We did everything we were supposed to do with stopping my death in the past from happening again. But now strange things are happening, and I don't think any of it is normal."

Alistair sat up straighter. "What kind of 'strange things?'"

"Birds have been ... threatening me," I said, not sure how else to word it. "The first one was at Drew's house. We were in his living room making s'mores, and then a bird—a crow—fell down the fireplace. It burned to death." The image of the feathers catching flame and the sad look in the crow's eyes as it gave up fighting for its life entered my mind again. I shivered at the memory.

"What else?" Alistair prodded me to continue.

I told him about the other two incidents—the birds crashing into my car last night, and the mob of them pecking at Drew's windows when we left school. It sounded like I was stuck in an old-time horror movie. The kind I refused to watch because they spooked me out to the extreme.

Hopefully Alistair would have answers.

"Before I tell you what I think this means, I want you to try recalling anything else out of the ordinary that's happened to you in the past few days," Alistair said. "I need as much information as possible before I can come to a conclusion."

I ran through recent events in my mind. Two things—disregarding the birds—stuck out. "My watch stopped," I said, motioning to the silver watch with the round face that Jeremy got me for my birthday last year. "I'm not sure if that counts as out of the ordinary, but I changed the battery last month, so it shouldn't have died so quickly. And then there were the pictures last night ..."

"The pictures?" Alistair raised a bushy eyebrow.

"Two framed pictures of me fell off the wall," I told him. "It didn't strike me as strange when it happened to the first one, except for how the nail wasn't broken. But when the second one fell after I put the first one back up ... I thought maybe it was a ghost."

"Not a ghost." Alistair sounded sure of what this meant. "It's something else."

"Do you want to elaborate?" Drew asked.

"I will, but you're not going to like what I'm about to say."

"I can handle it." My voice sounded steadier than I felt.

"I sensed something dark surrounding you when you walked into the store today," Alistair began. "And what you've told me confirms that my suspicions are correct. Someone has cast a curse on you."

I blinked a few times, unsure if I heard him right. "Come again?" I said. No way could he have said what I thought he did. Because reincarnation—I accepted that now. Soul mates, I've always believed in, so I accepted the truth there. But *curses*? That was extreme. There had to be a place where the line was drawn between fiction and reality, and a curse sounded way more on the fiction side of the spectrum.

"This isn't any old curse, either," Alistair continued. "It's been cast by someone with true magic in their blood, or someone who's received the rare gift of borrowing true magic."

"You need to back up." I raised my hands in a "stop" motion. Alistair sounded sure of this, but I didn't want to believe it was possible. "Why do you think I've been cursed?"

"What you've explained are dark omens." Alistair's voice was deeper now, more intense. He leaned forward, his eyes wild. "Omens of death. The crows, the watch, and the pictures ... it's quite clear. Someone has cast a strong curse on you; it surrounds your entire being. If you don't find out who's responsible and fix it ..." He looked away from us, as if he didn't want to say more.

Drew's fingers curled into a fist, so tight they turned white. "If we don't find out who's responsible and fix it, then what?" he asked, his voice tense.

"Then Lizzie will die," Alistair said simply.

I stared at the table, my chest empty. It hurt to breathe. I didn't want to believe this was possible. Hadn't I been through this already? Hadn't I already been doomed to die a violent death? And hadn't I stopped it so I could be a normal teenager from now on?

But something wasn't right, and Alistair had always been truthful with me.

"Why?" I asked, my voice cracking. "Why is this happening again?"

"This darkness wasn't around you when you visited on Saturday afternoon, so my guess is that between then and now, someone with magic who is very angry at you decided to retaliate."

"But I don't know anyone who has ... magic," I said, the word sounding ridiculous. "I'm not even sure if magic exists!"

"Oh, it does exist," Alistair said. "And I only know one person who has it. Or at least one who lives here."

"And who is that?" Drew asked, tapping his foot on the wooden floor. I could tell it was hard for him to be patient, but he seemed more accepting of this explanation than I was.

Then again, how else could I explain the crows, and the dark feeling I couldn't shake? Maybe it wouldn't hurt to go along with this and see what happened.

"Genevieve." Alistair's eyes darkened when he said her name.

"Who's Genevieve?" I asked. The name sounded old-fashioned. It was one I would remember if I'd met her before.

"Genevieve has been connected to me and my brother Tristan for all our lives," Alistair said. "She's shown up in each of our incarnations. She loves Tristan, and she blames me for his death."

"So you think Genevieve did this?" Drew's eyes blazed with anger.

"I believe Genevieve hates me enough to want to get back at me and make me fail as a Guide." Alistair raised his index finger to his lips, as though he were deep in thought. "But this curse ... it's very dark. And very strong. It's the kind of curse that can only be successful if the person casting it is emotionally close to their intended victim. Perhaps, in your case, someone who was close to you in your past life as well."

"Meaning it can't be Genevieve," I concluded.

"Correct," Alistair said. "It would have to be someone close to you who felt vulnerable enough, and angry enough, to be enticed by Genevieve to do her bidding."

Chelsea and Jeremy popped into my mind, although I suspected one more than the other. "I know some people who that could be," I said, although I didn't think either of them hated me enough to want me *dead*. They were hurt and upset by what I'd done to them—and rightly so—but to be so angry that they didn't want me to live? I'd known both of them for years, and neither of them could want that. It was too extreme. Too violent. Too ... evil.

I shuddered to think that either of them could do such a thing.

"Chelsea or Jeremy," Drew said in disgust.

I nodded. "But I don't know how to bring it up to either of them. Do I just walk up and say, 'Hey, did you cast a curse on me on Saturday or Sunday?'" I ran my fingers through my hair, feeling defeated. "And if they did do it—which I find hard to believe they hate me enough to do—why would they admit it? Wouldn't it be easier to let the curse work, to wait until ..."

Until I'm dead, I thought, unable to say the words aloud.

"No." Drew's voice was steady. "We're not going to allow that to happen. We'll get one of them to admit it, and then we'll make them reverse it."

"About that." Alistair cleared his throat, balancing one hand on his cane. I could tell I wasn't going to like what he was about to say. "Once a curse is cast, it's irreversible."

Any inkling of hope I'd felt before was sucked out of me.

I was doomed.

"But there are other ways to fix this," Alistair said before Drew or I could panic more than we already had. "Once we find out who did this, and exactly what they did, there will be a way—some way—to fix it. We'll just have to think outside the box."

"For sure?" I asked, my voice sounding small. "Or are you just saying that?"

"There are ways to do these things." His wrinkly grey eyes met mine, and I could tell he meant it. "Magic works in cycles, so the darkness won't have complete hold over you until the next full moon. Since last night was a full moon, that gives us a month to figure this out."

"What do you mean, it doesn't have complete hold of me?" I asked cautiously.

"Magic takes time to work," he explained. "It works in tune with the cycles of the moon. Right now it's simmering. Surrounding you, learning about you, scaring you. Gathering strength as it feeds off your fear. It won't be able to do what it was called on for until it's at its full power. We just have to figure out how to stop it before the next full moon. Which is, I believe, on Christmas day."

"It could have killed her when those birds hit her car last night," Drew muttered.

"It didn't, though." I rubbed the top of his hand with my thumb, trying to be reassuring. "I was fine."

"This time," he said, the muscles in his face tightening with determination. "But we need to stop this, and we need to stop it now."

"I agree," Alistair said. "And we can. But you must focus on the task at hand."

"Figuring out who did this to me, and getting the details on exactly what they did," I repeated what he'd told us earlier. "Then we can come up with a way to fix it."

It sounded simple when put that way. But I had an awful feeling that if Jeremy or Chelsea were responsible, there was no way I could get either of them to admit it.

CHAPTER 8

I decided to approach Jeremy first. It wasn't because I suspected him the most, but because I was afraid to talk to Chelsea—if I could even get her to talk to me, which I wasn't sure I would be able to do. At least if it was obvious Jeremy wasn't responsible, I could eliminate him as a suspect and focus on getting Chelsea to admit her guilt. Process of elimination was a good thing, right?

Probably not when you're under a time crunch, but talking to Jeremy wouldn't take more than a day. We had the rest of the month to get to the bottom of this.

Well, we had the rest of the month to make all this go away. After I figured out who was responsible, I suspected that fixing what they did was going to be harder than getting them to admit to doing it.

"The best way for me to get Jeremy to be honest with me is to talk with him alone," I told Drew as we left the car repair shop.

"No." He shook his head. "I don't like that. I should be there, too."

I got it, I did—no guy wants his girlfriend to be alone with the guy she just got out of a long-term relationship with. I hated knowing that Chelsea had stopped over Drew's on Sunday before I got there—even though he told her he loved me and kicked her out—and their relationship hadn't even been serious. I couldn't imagine how much harder it would be for Drew knowing I would be alone with Jeremy.

"I want you to be there too, but Jeremy will be more likely to admit he did something if he's just talking to me," I said. "If it's both of us, he might feel ganged up on."

"Or maybe he'll be more likely to admit to it under pressure," Drew said.

"But I don't think Jeremy's the one responsible," I replied. "If any of this is even possible. Do you really believe that stuff Alistair told us about curses and magic?"

"I'm not sure." Drew shrugged and looked at me, the vulnerability in his eyes taking me by surprise. "But it's all we have to go on right now, and I will do anything if it means keeping you safe."

The raw honesty in his statement took my breath away. "Thank you," I said. "I'll try to get Jeremy to meet at Starbucks, so there will be other people around. But I really do think it will be best if you sit this conversation out and let me handle him."

"Promise me you'll come over right when you're done?" he asked.

"I promise." I didn't need to think about my response.

"You'll need a car, though," Drew said. "Since yours won't be ready for a few days. You can take the Hummer."

"The Hummer?" I widened my eyes. "That thing is huge! How am I supposed to drive it?"

"You drive it just like any other car." Drew laughed. "You'll be fine. With everything going on, it makes me feel better to know you're in one of the safest cars on the road."

"Fine," I gave in. With Death after me, it made sense to drive the sturdiest car possible.

Although I suspected that once Death gained its full hold, a small thing like a car wouldn't stand in its way.

* * *

Jeremy agreed to meet me at Starbucks after his soccer practice. We used to go there a lot when we were dating, so the neutral territory would be a good place for us to talk.

I only hoped other people wouldn't listen to our conversation. It would sound pretty strange.

All day at school I could tell Jeremy was curious about what I wanted to talk with him about. He kept looking at me with hope in his eyes, and it made me feel bad. I didn't want him to think this had anything to do with "us"—that I wanted to get back together. The last thing I wanted was to hurt him more than I already had.

But I needed answers.

I did my homework at Starbucks while I waited for him, since I had time to kill between school and when his practice got out.

"I've been wondering all day what you wanted to talk with me about," Jeremy's voice brought me out of the essay I was writing for European History.

I looked up from my laptop—I couldn't believe I was so focused on writing that I hadn't seen him come in. He had showered after practice, so his sandy-blond hair was wet and darker than usual. He stuck his sunglasses into the front pocket of his jeans (I always told him he would smoosh them one day, but he never listened to me), and slid into the seat across from me. His cheeks were flushed—they always got like that when he finished soccer practice—and he watched me with his familiar blue eyes. The eyes I'd looked into every day until breaking up with him a few weeks ago.

I was right in breaking up with him, but I still felt awful about it. Despite the arrogant way he'd been acting since being voted co-captain of the varsity soccer team, Jeremy was basically a good guy. Maybe he wasn't completely considerate of others, but he never did anything with the intention of hurting someone. I trusted that given a few years, he would mature and become more thoughtful. Someday he would make a great boyfriend to someone—but that someone wasn't going to be me.

I closed my laptop, unsure how to begin.

"So, what's up?" Jeremy asked, taking a swig of the yellow Gatorade he brought in with him. He loved his sports drinks after a work out.

I sipped my tea, contemplating where to start.

"I just wanted to catch up," I said, willing my voice not to betray my anxiety. "With all the recent changes, I wanted to make sure things were okay between us. Since we were friends before we started dating, and now we're not together anymore ..." I wrung my hands together, unsure where I was going with this. I had to get to the point. "I wanted to make sure you're not angry with me."

"You get so cute when you're worried about something," he said with a laugh.

"Jere," I said, frustrated. "I'm serious. If you're angry at me ..."

"I'm not angry at you," he said, and I could tell by the warmness in his eyes that he meant it. "Sure, I'm bummed things didn't work between us, but I've done some thinking over the past few days."

I sat back and raised an eyebrow. Jeremy wasn't the pensive, deep thought type. "Thinking about what?" I asked.

"When you first broke up with me, yeah, I was angry," he said. "And when I realized you broke up with me because you wanted to be with Drew, I was even angrier."

"I didn't break up with you because of Drew," I said. "He was part of it, but there were other reasons. Drew just made me realize that some of those things that were wrong in our relationship didn't have to be that way."

"I know, I know." He held up a hand, letting me know he wanted to continue. "But I was thinking about it, and

I realized this was all going to happen eventually, anyway."

My lips parted in surprise. "What do you mean?"

"We're only juniors in high school, Liz. After graduation we're going to college, and we both know we won't end up in the same place. I want a big sports school, like Arizona or Maryland or Florida, and you want one of those small liberal arts places."

"True." I nodded, wondering where he was going with this.

"Four years in different states?" Jeremy shrugged and pushed his hair off his forehead. "We would see each other over breaks, but that wouldn't be enough. When I thought about it that way, I realized we would probably break up before the first semester ended. So yeah, I'm bummed it had to happen the way it did, but I'm not going to let it get to me. Plus, it helps to know that you respected me enough to end things with us before letting anything happen with ... anyone else." I could tell he didn't want to say Drew's name, which I understood. Just because Jeremy seemed to be forgiving me didn't mean he had to like Drew.

"You're not angry?" I asked, needing to know for sure. I couldn't believe Jeremy was taking this so well. He was a go with the flow sort of guy, but I hadn't expected him to get over our three year relationship this fast.

"No." He smiled, and I could tell he meant it. "Disappointed we couldn't be together longer, yeah. No one likes being broken up with. But no ... I'm not angry at you."

"Good." I breathed a sigh of relief. "I'm glad you told me this, Jere. I hated feeling weird around you in French and when I saw you in the cafeteria and stuff."

"Well, I'm glad you won't feel weird around me anymore," he said. "Does this mean you'll start coming to the soccer games again?" He smirked, and I could tell he was joking.

"Don't get your hopes up," I said with a laugh. "As you know, watching sports isn't my favorite activity. Especially now that it's almost December." I rubbed my hands over my arms, feeling cold just thinking about it.

"I didn't think so," he said. "But hey, do you think your friend Keelie is into me?"

"Keelie?" I hadn't seen that one coming. "I thought you were interested in Amber."

"Amber's all right, if you like the clingy, ditzy type," he said. "But she's already getting annoying."

"I'll ask Keelie," I told him, starting to wonder myself. Could Keelie be interested in Jeremy? I'd never stopped to think about it, but maybe she could be. And the two of them might be good together.

"Be smooth about it," he said, bringing his hands dramatically to his chest. "I don't want my heart to get broken again."

I smiled and rolled my eyes, glad that Jeremy was back to his normal, joking self. "I'll try to find out," I said. "And I really am glad things are cool between us now."

"No reason they shouldn't be," he said, like it was the easiest thing in the world.

"Right," I agreed, although "process of elimination" kept repeating in my mind. Because if Jeremy wasn't angry, there would be no reason for him to cast a curse on me.

Meaning only one person could be responsible—Chelsea.

CHAPTER 9

"What did Jeremy say?" Drew asked as he played with a ringlet of my hair that he found to be particularly bouncy.

"It wasn't him." I leaned back onto the headboard of Drew's bed and glanced at the plasma screen TV on his wall playing old episodes of The OC. We weren't really watching, but having the show on made sure Drew's mom didn't think we were doing anything in his room that our parents wouldn't approve of.

"How can you be sure?" Drew's eyes darkened in concern.

"I just am," I told him. "I wish you could have heard what he said. I don't even think he's upset about the break up anymore. He had this revelation that our relationship wouldn't have made it through us going to different colleges, so now he's fine with it. He even asked me to find out if Keelie's interested in him."

"He's interested in Keelie?" Drew looked perplexed.

"Yeah," I said. "I was surprised too, but it makes sense. Keelie and I are similar, but unlike me, she likes going to sports games and all that school spirit stuff."

"Hm," he said. "When you put it that way, it does kind of make sense."

"Anyway, that's not the point," I tried to get the conversation back to what we needed to discuss. "Because now that we know Jeremy isn't responsible, I need to talk to Chelsea."

"I thought it was her since Alistair told us about the curse," Drew said. "You know she's not going to admit it, right?"

"That's what I'm most worried about." I chewed on my lower lip. "I was just going to try talking with her and see what happens."

"The best chance you have is to catch her with evidence, so she can't deny it," he said simply.

I took a moment to absorb his words. I hoped he had a plan, because I sure didn't. "How do you suppose I do that?"

"Thanksgiving dinner." He sat up straighter, and I suspected he'd been thinking about this all day. "You're going over her house."

"What do you want me to do when I'm there?" I asked. "Raid her room?"

He raised an eyebrow, giving me the feeling that yes, that was exactly what he wanted me to do.

"No." I shook my head. "No way. Not happening."

"Why not?" he asked. "We agreed she's not going to admit it if you ask nicely. If it ends up making a difference between you staying alive or not, isn't it worth it to peek through her stuff?"

I pressed my lips together, not saying anything. I'd never snooped through anyone's stuff before. Just thinking about it felt intrusive.

"Have you had any more dark omens today?" he asked.

"The mirror in my bronzer compact cracked when I was getting ready for school," I admitted.

"Broken mirror," he said. "If that's not an obvious sign, then I don't know what is."

"It's not like I need these signs." I pulled my legs up to my chest and wrapped my arms around them, like a barrier to the bad luck surrounding me. "We already know about the death omens. There's no need to keep being reminded about it. It's like whatever's trying to get me is torturing me first. I hate it."

He put his arms around me and pulled me closer, so my cheek rested on his chest. I listened to the steady sound of his heartbeat and considered his suggestion. It wasn't like I questioned if Chelsea was responsible or not. It had to be her—it was the only possibility that made sense. And while I hated the idea of sneaking through Chelsea's room, wasn't it worth it if I found something that forced her to admit what she did? Then we could figure out how to fix this mess she'd created.

What was a little privacy intrusion compared to putting a curse on me that resulted in omens of death teasing me until they could do their dirty work a month from now?

Which led to the issue bothering me most: I understood that Chelsea was angry with me, and that she might never want to be friends with me again. Maybe I didn't deserve her friendship after not being honest with her about my feelings for Drew. But to hate me so much that she wanted me *dead*?

Chelsea wasn't the sweetest person in the world, but I never thought she could be that ... evil.

"Are you okay?" Drew asked, bringing me out of my thoughts.

I realized a tear had slipped out, and I tried to wipe it away before he saw it.

"Hey," he said, cupping my cheeks his hands. "We're not going to let anything bad happen to you, okay?"

Looking into his brown, gold-flecked eyes, full of emotion for every word he was saying, I knew he meant it. Together we would do everything possible to stop this spell from taking effect.

And if we were truly going to do everything possible, it meant doing things I wouldn't do in normal circumstances—like raiding my former best friend's room when I was over her house for Thanksgiving dinner.

"I don't like thinking that Chelsea could hate me enough to do this." I sniffed. "But I do see why your idea might work."

"So you'll do it?"

"I'll do it," I confirmed. "We just have to figure out how I can avoid getting caught. At least not until I find something useful."

With that, we formulated a plan.

CHAPTER 10

Every Thanksgiving up to this one, I'd woken up relaxed, knowing I didn't have to worry about homework since our teachers never assigned it over break. The scent of pancakes would filter through my room—my mom cooked them every Thanksgiving morning—and I would have a bunch of texts from friends, mostly mass text messages wishing me a Happy Thanksgiving.

All of that was the same today, minus the feeling relaxed part.

This morning, I was so worried about what was going to happen at dinner that not even the delicious smell of pancakes was making me hungry.

I rolled over and clutched my comforter tighter around me, not wanting to wake up. Why was it that when you were looking forward to a specific day, it took forever to arrive, but when you were dreading a day, it was there immediately?

I wanted to close my eyes and sleep more, so I wouldn't have to think about the upcoming task tonight. The idea of being in confined quarters with Chelsea was making me nauseated.

"Elizabeth!" my mom called from downstairs. "Time for breakfast!"

I managed to get out of bed, trudge to the bathroom, and freshen up before heading downstairs. I looked awful—the huge circles under my eyes were a giveaway to how long it had taken me to fall asleep last night.

"You look exhausted," my mom said when I stepped into the kitchen. "Trouble sleeping?"

"I haven't talked to Chelsea since trying to apologize on Saturday," I said, setting the table in preparation for the Thanksgiving Breakfast Pancake Feast. "And that didn't go well."

"You're worried about seeing her tonight," my mom guessed. I doubted it was hard to figure out.

"Yeah." I nodded. "She won't talk to me at school anymore. Luckily I have Drew and Keelie and Hannah—even Jeremy and I are on good terms now—but I miss being friends with Chelsea."

I'd actually talked with Keelie about the same thing Tuesday at lunch. She didn't understand why I wanted to be friends with Chelsea in the first place. She said Chelsea was an awful friend, and that people at school thought she was snobby. I wondered if people thought I was snobby for hanging out with her, but I didn't ask. It's amazing how often people mistake shyness for snobbiness.

All it took to make Keelie understand was reminding her that she had been best friends with Shannon since elementary school. Shannon made Chelsea look tame. Sometimes the history you had with someone was more important than anything else. The sleepovers in middle school when we did each other's makeup and watched made-for-TV movies all night, the time when Chelsea stood up for me when people made fun of me in French class last year, and all the time talking on the phone chatting about whatever was on our minds. You grew comfortable with that person. They knew everything about you, the good and the bad, and wanted to spend time with you anyway.

That sort of friendship isn't something you can walk away from without caring at all.

"Are you sure you're okay going over there?" my mom asked, placing a stack of pancakes in the center of the table and sitting down. "I could tell Tyler you weren't feeling well."

I wished that were possible. If I didn't have to investigate Chelsea's room, I probably would have agreed to it. And it wouldn't have been a lie, since the idea of being around Chelsea was truly making me feel sick.

"No, it's okay," I told my mom, forcing a smile. "It might be a good thing to see Chelsea away from school."

"Maybe she'll get into the spirit of Thanksgiving and will want to forgive you and start fresh," my mom said, putting two pancakes onto her plate.

I did the same, figuring I should try to eat. "That would be nice, but I don't think so."

"You never know," she said. "It *is* the most magical time of the year."

"That's Christmas, Mom." I rolled my eyes.

"And the spirit of Christmas starts on Thanksgiving!" she argued. "Speaking of which, I have to give the handyman a call this week so he can get our lights up."

That was one big similarity between my mom and I— we were indoor girls. Neither of us climbed ladders in the freezing cold to wrestle with Christmas lights.

Hopefully I wouldn't be stuck doing Christmas dinner with Chelsea and her dad, too. That would really be awful. I figured it was best not to say anything.

Who knew what could happen between now and then?

* * *

Once I started eating pancakes, they were so good that I'd had way more than I should have. I didn't know how I would be hungry for dinner. My mom and I did our Thanksgiving tradition of watching the Macy's Day Parade in the living room, followed by the dog show that was on afterward. The dogs were cute to watch, although I was more of a cat person. Not that I could get a cat while I lived at home, since my mom was allergic, but I planned on getting one after graduating college.

That was a long way off, though. And I shouldn't be planning that far ahead, since my biggest concern right now was fixing whatever dark spell Chelsea did so I would make it through the next full moon.

My mom and I weren't into sports, so we didn't watch the football game, despite it being an American tradition.

Instead, I took a long, hot shower, and spent a lot of time getting ready for dinner. I wanted to look my best. Yes, it was only Chelsea and her dad, but by looking good, I could give Chelsea the impression that her being mad at me wasn't stressing me out as much as it was.

I wore a new dress, and blew out my hair and straightened it, which I hadn't done for months. Mainly because straightening my hair reminded me of how Jeremy had pushed me to wear it straight because he liked it better that way. But I liked how my hair looked both curly and straight, and I was no longer the girl who wore my hair a certain way because my boyfriend told me to. I would do whatever I was in the mood for.

Drew would tell me I looked beautiful no matter how I wore my hair, even if I did something crazy like chop it all off. I would never do something like that, but knowing he wouldn't judge me for it was important.

The day passed fast. When we arrived at Chelsea's, I looked at the house I'd been to a million times—wooden panels, blue shutters, the two car garage, and the brick chimney.

I had so many good memories there, but right now, all I could feel was dread.

CHAPTER 11

To say that dinner was awkward would be the understatement of the past two centuries. At least my mom and Chelsea's dad were low-key about their relationship. I think they were trying to make Chelsea and me comfortable. I couldn't speak for Chelsea, but I was grateful for that.

Chelsea one-upped me with outfits for the night, wearing a red dress that hugged her curves, and was short without being inappropriate for a family dinner. She'd also put on a lot of makeup—thick black eyeliner, and her lips were painted in the same dark red she'd been wearing to school for the past week.

If she had cast a curse on me, she was certainly getting into the part.

I would have busied myself by helping set the table and getting the food ready—anything to avoid Chelsea—but Mr. Givens had hired his housekeeper to help, so none of that was necessary. Instead, I was in the living room, drinking sparkling cider from a champagne flute while my mom and Mr. Givens had glasses of wine. Chelsea had a champagne flute of cider as well. I would have been fine with a normal glass, but I think Mr. Givens wanted us to feel grown up. It didn't matter to me, but Chelsea kept toying with the stem, like she was at a fancy function instead of in the living room with the three of us. Every so often she would glance longingly at the bottle of wine, and I knew she would have preferred that to the cider.

I wasn't into drinking, but at this point I imagined a glass or two of white wine would make me a lot less nervous for what I had to do tonight.

Every time my eyes met Chelsea's, her gaze hardened, and her lips curled into a sneer. I wondered if my mom noticed. At least Mr. Givens had the foresight to have music playing in the background. It made the silences less awkward. There weren't many silences, though—my mom and Mr. Givens kept up the chit-chat nicely.

After what felt like hours (but was really only thirty minutes), we headed to the table to eat dinner. I didn't know how I was hungry after the Pancake Feast that morning, but the moment I inhaled the comforting smell of Thanksgiving food, my stomach rumbled. Neither Chelsea's dad nor my mom cooked, so they ordered the food in from a local restaurant, and it smelled delicious.

But since the plan was set to start during dinner, the sight of the table worried me. Was I really about to do this? The plan wasn't complicated, but it could still go wrong. I could get caught. And if I got caught ... what could I possibly say?

Hopefully I wouldn't get caught.

Luckily no one insisted we do that activity before dinner where each person says something they're thankful for. Chelsea would have sneered or laughed at whatever I had to say. Plus, I was most thankful for Drew entering my life and changing everything; for being lucky enough to have met my soul mate.

If I said that aloud, Chelsea might rip my head off.

Mid-way through dinner, I excused myself, presumably to use the restroom. But that wasn't my actual destination. I'd been over Chelsea's house enough times to know that the powder room was near the stairs, which led up to Chelsea's bedroom.

My stomach flipped at the thought of what I was about to do. Hopefully it wouldn't be hard to find what I needed in Chelsea's room. I didn't want to be gone for too long and have everyone wonder if I was okay.

The worst that could happen was that they would assume I wasn't feeling well. It would be embarrassing, but worth it if I found what I needed.

When I got to the powder room, I opened and closed the door in the pretense of going in. I was probably being paranoid—I doubted they could hear it from the dining room—but it made me feel better. Then I slipped off my shoes and held them as I hurried up the wooden steps. My heart was pounding, but I did my best to calm down by focusing on the task at hand. If I let my mind wander, I would only feel guilty about what I was doing. I couldn't afford to be distracted.

Besides, Chelsea had a lot more to feel guilty about if she'd cursed me to die.

Once inside her room, I turned on the lights, set my shoes down on her vacuumed white carpet, and looked around. Chelsea was a neat freak, so nothing was out of place.

If only I knew where to start. Her four-poster bed was made without a crease on it, her makeup was organized in perfect lines on her vanity, and her desk was sectioned off so everything was in its proper place. The items on her desk looked the same as when I was over on Saturday—except for the candle next to her laptop. A round, squat red candle that judging from the small amount of wax burned away on the top, had only been used once.

In all the time I'd known Chelsea, she'd never had a candle in her room, let alone lit one. What were the chances that she had purchased one—and used it—within the time frame that someone close to me had cast a curse on me?

This couldn't be a coincidence.

I also doubted that telling Chelsea I found her candle was going to be enough evidence to make her admit to what she did. I needed more proof if I wanted her cornered.

Which led to the next step of Drew's plan—check out what websites Chelsea had been browsing recently. If I found something incriminating, something relating to magic and spells, it would point to Chelsea being responsible for casting the curse.

I opened her laptop, glad it wasn't password protected, and went straight to her web browser. The majority of her recent history was Facebook. The worst part was that when I looked closer, she was obviously stalking Drew's page. She especially loved looking at any photo of the two of them together. She also visited his Twitter multiple times, even though he barely updated it.

Knowing that my ex-best friend had feelings for my boyfriend? I didn't like that, and I wished things didn't have to be that way. Knowing she followed his every move online? I'm not going to be a hypocrite, because everyone's done their share of Internet stalking, but it was different seeing it in front of me. And it definitely annoyed me. There was a part of me that wished Drew wasn't Facebook friends with her, but de-friending someone was petty, and caused unnecessary drama. Anyway, Chelsea looking at his page wasn't hurting anything.

But if my instincts were correct, she *had* done something to hurt me.

I had to figure out what that something was.

Reminded of the reason I was searching through her computer, I looked further back into her browser's history. Nothing stuck out from yesterday or the day before that.

Then I reached Sunday night, and froze at the titles of the visited web pages:

Remembering past lives.

Past life regression—Wikipedia.
Spells to make him fall in love with you.
Free love spells guaranteed to work.

The list continued—pages and pages of research into past lives and love spells. I imagined most of them were tacky and way off from the truth, but perhaps she'd found something that worked. After all, when I first suspected I was remembering a past life, I'd done online research. Most of the websites were ridiculous, but a few of them weren't terrible.

If the magic sites were the same way, Chelsea could have found a spell that worked.

Then I remembered what Alistair had said about her having to drink witch's blood to cast such a dark curse. I couldn't imagine Chelsea doing something so repulsive. So could she be a witch? I doubted it, but if the curse worked, then maybe she was.

I continued to look through the history of the browser, amazed by how many sites she'd visited. She must have gotten barely any sleep Sunday night.

Suddenly the door flew open.

I sat back in the chair, staring wide-eyed at Chelsea as she crossed her arms and leered at me from the doorway.

"What are you doing in my room?" she asked with so much malice that it sounded like she wanted to kill me on the spot.

CHAPTER 12

My hands hovered over the keyboard of her MacBook Air, caught in the act. I had a feeling that "I had an urge to check my e-mail" wouldn't be an acceptable explanation. Which was too bad, because I couldn't think of anything else.

It looked like "The Confrontation" was going to happen right here, right now.

"Well?" Chelsea's voice was full of ice.

Despite the guilt building in my chest, I reminded myself of the reasons I was here. Chelsea had cast a *curse* on me. She wanted me dead. That was way worse than my snooping in her room. Plus, I'd found what I was looking for. She was the one at fault—not me.

I forced myself to hold her gaze. "You should be the one explaining why you cast a curse to kill me."

At first she looked guilty, but then her expression turned to shock. "I did no such thing," she insisted.

"Really?" I raised an eyebrow. "Because what I found in your browsing history suggests otherwise."

"I have no idea what you're talking about," she continued to deny her actions, although she shut the door so our parents couldn't overhear. Then she walked over to her desk and slammed the laptop shut, her eyes wide with fury. "You have no right to be looking through my things. You shouldn't be here at all, but it's not like I had any say in the matter. I was hoping you would fake sick so you didn't have to come to dinner. That's what you *should* have done. You lying, boyfriend stealing, little brat."

I stared at her in amazement. I knew she was mad at me, but that was a hateful thing to say. My eyes filled with tears, and I blinked them away, but not before one slipped out.

"The most pathetic thing is that you thought I would still want to be friends with you," Chelsea continued, her voice escalating in volume. "Coming in here the day after Shannon's party and saying how you and Drew were meant to be together, that you were soul mates, and that you loved him, blah, blah, blah. Well, here's some news for you, Lizzie. Drew was supposed to end up with me, not you. You messed everything up. All I've done is try to fix my life and make it the way it was supposed to be before you destroyed it!"

"Fix your life?" I repeated, my head swimming with confusion. "What do you mean, that Drew was supposed to end up with you and I 'destroyed it?'"

"You know what I mean." She sneered. "When this happened the first time, Drew ended up with me. That's what was supposed to happen. Not him choosing you. It's all wrong, and I had to set things right."

I couldn't believe she thought that. And if what she was saying was true, then she had gotten flashes of the past, too.

But how was that possible?

"What do you remember?" I asked.

"Enough." She huffed.

"So you've had flashes of the past? You remember who we were back then?"

"You mean the past life we all had together in Regency Era, England, when I married Drew?" Chelsea said. "Because if that's what you mean, then yes, I've had flashes of the past. I remember what happened then. Drew married me. He *chose* me."

"That can't be right." I felt dizzy with everything she was throwing at me. Drew had never told me what happened to his past self after my death. Could he have married Catherine—Chelsea's past self? His parents back then wanted him to marry her for her noble title, so with my past self dead, he might have gone through with it to please them.

"Oh, but it is right," Chelsea said. "I saw it."

"When?" I asked, shocked that she remembered anything at all. According to Alistair, to get flashes people needed a trigger. My trigger was Drew. What was Chelsea's? "When did you remember?"

"Probably after you," she said. "Because I'm getting the feeling that you remembered before I did. Way before I did. Not that I'm surprised you didn't tell me." She flipped her shiny, auburn hair over her shoulder. "You've been quite the secretive one lately, haven't you?"

Chelsea had somehow made it sound like everything was my fault, even though she was wrong. This wasn't how this conversation was supposed to go. I had to gain control. I was on a mission: Find out what she'd done, and fix it.

"Would you have believed me if I'd told you?" I said, gaining courage when she didn't say yes. "I began getting the flashes shortly after meeting Drew, when he walked into our History class on the first day of school. I remembered my past life gradually; I wasn't sure it was real at first. But what I remembered was clear—in the past, Drew broke up with you to be with me. So from what you're saying, there were clearly some differences with what we saw."

"I would love to hear what was so different that you couldn't understand what it meant that Drew *married* me!" Chelsea said, her hands curled into fists. "What's hard to understand about that? Clearly I'm the one he wanted to be with!"

"He would have married me if I hadn't died before he had the chance," I said flatly.

That stopped Chelsea in her tracks.

"But you didn't see that part, did you?"

She looked stunned, and unsure how to respond.

Of course my mom chose that moment to stick her head through the door.

"Is everything all right up here?" she asked, her forehead creased as she looked back and forth between us. I guessed they could hear Chelsea's yelling from downstairs.

"It's fine." I managed to smile. "Chelsea and I just have some stuff to talk about, if that's okay."

"I understand," she said. "Tyler said he would have come up, but he thought I was more suited to deal with 'girl stuff.' Take as much time as you need. We'll wait for you for dessert."

She slipped out of the room and closed the door, leaving Chelsea and me alone.

Not wanting Chelsea to put me on the defensive again, I took control of the conversation. "We need to compare what we saw in our flashbacks," I said. "Clearly we're both missing important information. It'll be good to piece everything together so we can figure this out."

Hopefully Chelsea wasn't so angry that she would refuse to approach this logically. My mom had always stressed to me that communication was key in any relationship. Chelsea and I were lacking in communication recently, and comparing memories seemed like the best way to start fixing this mess.

"If that will make you realize that Drew and I are supposed to be together, then fine." Chelsea stuck her chin defiantly in the air, although I had a feeling that something had changed when I mentioned my death in the past. She kicked off her shoes and walked to her bed, falling into it and leaning against her mountain of pillows. "I'll start."

I had wanted to start, since I got the flashes first, but I stayed quiet. Chelsea was cooperating, and I didn't want to mess that up.

"Before I start, you have to promise you won't repeat what I'm about to tell you to anyone," Chelsea said seriously, without a trace of the earlier anger in her tone. "If Shannon finds out I let you in on this, she'll be beyond angry."

"What does Shannon have to do with this?" I asked.

"Promise you won't tell anyone, and I'll tell you," Chelsea said.

I wouldn't keep what she told me from Drew, but since it wouldn't help to point that out, I agreed to her condition. I hated knowing I would go back on my promise the minute I talked to Drew tonight, but I tried not to dwell on it.

The small lie was worth it to save my life.

"Sunday morning, Shannon dragged me to that Mystic Pathways store in the mall," Chelsea said. "We went there once a few years ago. Remember?"

"Yeah." I nodded, remembering how we'd gone into the store as a joke. It was dark inside, and filled with herbs, crystals, and so-called magical candles. Then we saw the creepy old lady who worked there, looking like an evil character in a fairy tale. We bolted out of the store, and joked about her being a witch. I hadn't given that day much thought since.

"The lady who works there is Shannon's aunt, but that's not the point," Chelsea said with a wave of her hand. "The point is that she convinced me she could help me get Drew back, and she took me into the back room. She did some past life regression voodoo, and that's when it came back to me."

"Your past life?" I asked, gripping the armrests of the chair.

"The first thing I saw was Drew dancing with me at a ball." Chelsea's eyes took on a far-off look, like she was seeing the scene in front of her as she described it. "We were happy, and having fun. I saw you there too, but after I saw you, the scene switched to one of me and Drew talking in a garden. He looked upset—really upset—but I don't know what was wrong. All I know was that he was coming to me with his problem, and I was doing my best to help him get through whatever was troubling him. The next thing I knew, I was in a church watching myself marry Drew."

I didn't want to believe it was possible, but I doubted Chelsea had made that up. "Was I there?" I asked, trying to ignore how hurt I was at the possibility that Drew had married Catherine and not told me. Or maybe he just didn't remember. I didn't remember much about my past, either—only the parts with Drew. If he only remembered the parts when he was with me, then he wouldn't remember anything beyond my death.

"I don't know." Chelsea lifted a small pillow from the bed and hugged it. "It was pretty fuzzy. I saw some people in the crowd, but no, I don't remember seeing you."

"Because I was dead," I reminded her.

"Maybe." Her eyes darkened, like she didn't want to believe it.

Then I told her my side of the story. How after I saw Drew for the first time in European History, I felt like I knew him from somewhere, but couldn't place where that was. How soon afterwards, strange things started happening to me, like the sketches I'd made of my past self in Regency England, and becoming fluent in French. How Drew came to the Halloween dance, and when we danced together, I had a flashback of us dancing at the ball we attended in the past—the same ball I assumed Chelsea saw during her "regression session" at Mystic Pathways. I told her about meeting Alistair, his role as my Memory Guide, and how he gave me objects to help me remember my past life, like the mask, the necklace, the original printing of *Pride and Prejudice*, and the sheet music for "Minuet." I told her about remembering how to play piano as easily as I'd remembered how to speak French. Finally I told her about what happened the night of Shannon's party—the flash I had of Catherine and Drew together in the past, and the memory of the carriage accident that had ended in my death.

Surprisingly, she listened to everything without interruption.

"So in the past ... you died," Chelsea said once I finished. She sounded like she didn't want to believe it was true.

"Yes," I confirmed. "And when I was in the car with Jeremy after Shannon's party, I stopped the past from repeating itself. But on Sunday night, something changed. Creepy things started happening to me, like crows attacking me, my watch stopping, and pictures falling off the walls. Drew and I went to Alistair the next day to ask what it meant. Alistair said they were death omens, because someone who was close to me in the past had cast a curse on me. He said ..." I swallowed, preparing to say the terrifying thing that would happen if everything continued on its current path. "He said if I didn't find out who cast the curse, and exactly what they did, I'm going to die by the next full moon. That's why I was sneaking around in your room. I had to know if it was you. Wouldn't you have done the same thing if you were me?"

Chelsea played with the edges of the pillow, looking terribly guilty. "I didn't want you to die," she said, looking up to meet my eyes. "I was angry about everything that happened, and I'm still mad at you for not being honest with me from the beginning and for spending time with Drew behind my back. But when I said in the spell that I wanted things to end the same way they did in our past lives, I thought it meant that Drew and I would be together. I didn't realize it meant you would die. We've been friends forever, Lizzie. You know I'm not that bad of a person."

"I know." I played with the chain heart bracelet Drew had given me as I gathered my thoughts. "But whatever you did, even if you didn't do it on purpose, it's done now. You can't take it back."

"We can't reverse it?"

"No." I shook my head. "Once a spell is cast, it's irreversible. By the way," I said, "how long have you known you were ... a witch?" I laughed, because despite the seriousness of the conversation, I still had a hard time believing witches existed.

"I don't think I *am* a witch," Chelsea said. "If I am, the only reason I know is because the spell worked."

"Alistair said the only other way for you to do a spell would be if you drank a witch's blood." I wrinkled my nose at the prospect. "Even if you wanted the spell to work more than anything you've wanted in your life, that's gross. I know you wouldn't agree to that."

Chelsea paled, her expression changing to one of horror and disgust.

"You didn't." I gasped. "Did you?"

"Genevieve gave me a vial of red liquid to drink," she said. "But I know what blood looks like, and it wasn't close to thick enough. It was the consistency of water."

"All you would have needed was a drop," I told her what Alistair had told Drew and me earlier that week. "And Alistair warned me about Genevieve. She's the witch who's mad at him because of something that happened in their past lives. He suspected she was behind this."

"I can't believe I drank someone's blood." Chelsea held her hands up to her throat, her eyes wide in revulsion. "That's so gross."

"It is," I agreed. "But it explains why you could do the spell."

"I need water," she said. She got up, hurried to the second floor bathroom, and turned on the faucet. A minute later, she returned with a cup of water. She took a few sips, and some color returned to her cheeks.

"Now that we know you're responsible for the death omens, you should come with me and Drew when we see Alistair," I said. I understood she was having issues with the drinking blood realization, but we had bigger problems to deal with. "I'm right in assuming you want to help us fix this, right?"

"Yes." She placed the now finished cup of water on her nightstand. "I'll definitely help. I honestly didn't think ..." She looked straight at me, her eyes glassy, like she might cry. "Please believe me that I didn't think what I did would kill you. I thought that because Drew and I were together in the past it meant something went wrong in the present, and that what I was doing was setting things back on track. If I'd known it meant you would die, I never would have done it. I wouldn't have *considered* it."

"I believe you," I said. "But we have to focus. Drew and I are going to the mall tomorrow to talk to Alistair. Will you come with us?"

"You realize the mall's going to be a zoo tomorrow, right?" Chelsea asked. "Since it's Black Friday?" She shuddered, and I couldn't help but laugh. Chelsea and I always boycotted Black Friday—I didn't like crowds, and she didn't think the deals were worth the annoyance of waiting in long lines.

"We don't have loads of time here," I pointed out. "Only until the next full moon. Are you coming or not?"

"If it means saving you from an untimely death that I accidentally caused?" Chelsea asked, raising a perfectly plucked eyebrow. "Count me in."

I wasn't sure if we were back to being friends, but this was definitely a start.

CHAPTER 13

When I told Drew what Chelsea had done, he was furious. Then I clarified the situation, letting him know that Chelsea had no idea I died in the past, so she didn't know how extreme the results of her actions would be. After hearing that, he relaxed enough to listen to the rest of what I had to say.

I was most nervous about asking him if he married Catherine in the past after my death. That would be a big secret for him to keep, and I didn't want another confrontation. Luckily he didn't remember anything after my death, so he hadn't been keeping it secret, but he said it was possible he ended up with Catherine. His family back then was pushy with wanting the noble title. Without me, he said he would have felt like he had nothing to live for, so he might have gone through with the marriage to please his family.

I wasn't happy to hear that, but I did my best not to dwell on the past. What happened then was history. What mattered was fixing things in the present to make sure I would have a future.

* * *

After an awkward car ride with Drew and Chelsea, the three of us made it to the mall. The parking lot was packed. Luckily, a family was leaving when we got there, so we nabbed their spot near the front.

The mall was more crowded than I had ever seen it. Even Alistair's shop, which was normally pretty empty, was teeming with people high on the Black Friday Shopping Craze. He had hired extra help, though, so when he spotted Drew, Chelsea, and me, he ushered us to the back room so we could talk in private.

The room was small, with a table in the middle and books lining the shelves. He told us to sit, and got down to business.

"Who have you brought with you today?" he asked, looking pointedly at Chelsea.

I introduced her, and she brought him up to speed on what she had told me last night.

"This is going to be tricky," he said once she finished telling the story. "To help, I need to know exactly how you did the spell."

"No problem," Chelsea said. "Genevieve had me light the red candle she gave me and write on a piece of paper, 'I wish that everything in this life between me,

Drew, and Lizzie will end up the same way it did in our past lives.' Then I said it out loud and burned the paper."

"You did this after drinking her blood?" Alistair asked.

Chelsea paled at the mention of the blood-drinking. "Yes," she said. "But I didn't know it was blood. If I did, I never would have drank it. I thought it was water with red dye in it."

"What you thought doesn't matter," Alistair said, his eyes hard. "What matters is what you did."

"I didn't realize it was going to make Lizzie die," Chelsea pleaded, with tears in her eyes. "If I knew, there's no way I would have gone through with it."

"I believe you," I said, and I did. She nodded in acceptance of my words. Then I turned to Alistair. "We can fix this. Right?"

He contemplated the question, and I feared he was going to say it would be impossible. "I think we can," he said. "But it's not going to be easy."

Drew's eyes flashed with determination. "Tell us what we have to do, and we'll do it."

"When Chelsea cast the spell, she made it so the three of you would get the same endings you did in your past lives. Therefore, what Lizzie did last weekend by making sure the present didn't parallel the past doesn't matter." He took a breath, and continued, "The wording of the spell was specific: Your current lives will end the same way they did in the past. Since Lizzie died young in the past, she will be doomed to die young again."

That was what I figured when Chelsea explained the spell, but hearing it said aloud made it terrifyingly real.

"I understand that," Drew said. "But since spells can't be reversed, how are we going to fix it?"

"You will have to make it so Lizzie doesn't die young in the past," Alistair said simply.

"Hold up a minute." I couldn't believe what he'd said. "Are you saying that we can affect what happened in the past? That we can change it?"

"If you can manage to get there—and that's not going to be easy—then yes, you can change it."

I took a moment to make sure he meant what I thought he did. "So you're telling us we can ... travel back in time?" I couldn't believe the words coming out of my mouth. This was impossible. I could handle reincarnation, and I could wrap my mind around Chelsea drinking witch blood and casting a spell, but *time travel*?

That happened in science-fiction stories, not real life.

"This is nuts," Chelsea said what I was thinking.

"Yeah," I agreed. "If time travel were possible, wouldn't people from the future travel back in time to let us know?"

"It is possible," Alistair said. "Extremely difficult, but possible. And to answer your question, the reason we don't have visitors from the future is because if the three of you manage to travel back in time, you will experience that time from the bodies of your past selves. So when you are there, you must tell no one the truth, because if you do, they will think you have lost your minds."

This was out there, and I didn't believe it was possible, but I decided to put aside my skepticism and ask questions.

"How would we get there?" I asked. "I have a feeling it's going to be more complicated than clicking my heels together and wishing I was in 1815 England."

"Your feeling is correct," Alistair said.

"So how do we do it?" Drew asked.

"Come on." Chelsea shook her hair out and laughed. "You don't believe all this, do you?"

Drew glared at her. "If it gives us a chance to change what you did to Lizzie, then I'm willing to give it a shot."

Chelsea shrunk back at the reminder of what she'd done.

"You will need an object," Alistair started.

"What kind of 'object?'" Drew asked.

Alistair raised his eyebrows. "Are you going to let me continue or not?"

Drew nodded and leaned back in his seat.

"This object has to be powerful enough to transport you into the bodies of your past selves," Alistair said. "Therefore, it must have existed back then, so it knows the time period. It also must be something that's important to you in both the past and the present if it's going to make the link you need for the journey. It's preferable that the object is something a person would wear, as that makes it easier to pick up a person's aura. Any type of metal or gem works best. Can you think of anything that fits this description?"

"The ring," Drew and I said in unison.

"What ring?" Chelsea asked.

"In the past, on the day I died, Drew proposed to me in secret," I told her. "The ring had a gold band, and five garnets along the top."

Chelsea frowned. I could tell that hearing about the secret engagement hurt her, but keeping her feelings in tact wasn't my primary concern at the moment.

"Are you in possession of this ring?" Alistair asked.

"Well, no," I admitted. Then I looked at Drew, and said, "Unless you have it and were waiting for the right time to tell me."

"I wish I had it," he said. "So I could give it to you. But I have no idea where to start looking for it. You were wearing it when ..." He choked up, and then continued, "You were wearing it when you died. I don't remember anything from after then."

"You have no idea where it could be?" Alistair asked.

"No." Drew shook his head. "It could be anywhere."

CHAPTER 14

The one item that could get us to the past, and it could be anywhere.

This was not looking good.

Of course, this was assuming everything Alistair had said was possible. I trusted I had been reincarnated, because it was the only explanation that made the memories of my past life make sense. I knew Chelsea had cast the spell because of the omens, and because she had admitted it.

But there was no reason for me to believe we could travel back to 1815. It sounded crazy.

Then again, what other option did I have? If I didn't take action, I would die by the next full moon. I wasn't going to sit back and let that happen.

Alistair had been honest with me about everything so far. He wouldn't get my hopes up for nothing. Making this up would be a waste of time for all four of us.

No matter how crazy this idea sounded, I had to give it a shot.

"We will have to do a tracking spell," Alistair said.

"What's a tracking spell?" I asked, even though I could guess from the name.

"It will track the location of the ring," he replied.

"And this tracking spell will definitely work?"

"With Chelsea's help, and if the ring is in tact, then yes, it will work."

"Why do you need my help?" Chelsea asked.

"You drank the potion with Genevieve's blood on Sunday night, correct?" Alistair asked.

Chelsea nodded, grimacing at the mention of the potion. I couldn't blame her. It was gross that she drank that old woman's blood.

"That means Genevieve's power is still in your system," Alistair said. "You will be able to do magic until the next full moon, and we need magic to make the tracking spell work."

"She'll help," Drew said, looking at Alistair and not Chelsea. "After what she did, she owes us at least that much."

I got a feeling from the tense way Drew was speaking that it was going to be a long time before he forgave Chelsea—if he ever did. I was having difficulty with that myself, although I was trying not to think about it too much. What Chelsea did was awful, but she didn't intend to kill me. Still, that didn't stop me from being angry at her for doing it so recklessly, without understanding the possible consequences.

But I would worry about my reaction to what she did after making sure I lived past Christmas. Doing whatever I could to make the curse not end in my death was my top priority. Friendship drama would have to wait until later.

"How do you know so much about magic?" I asked Alistair. "Since you aren't a witch yourself."

"It's one of the many things I learned while training to be a Memory Guide," he replied. "We need to be able to help the Reincarnees the best way we can, and sometimes magic is necessary to do that. Like it is right now."

That made sense. Since I planned to become a Memory Guide once I passed on, I supposed that would be something I would learn in the future.

Hopefully the very *far* future.

"We don't have a lot of time," Drew said. "Let's get started. We can save the questions for after we know Lizzie's safe."

"Allow me to gather the needed materials," Alistair said. "And then we can begin."

CHAPTER 15

It took Alistair a few minutes to find what he needed and begin preparing the room. He opened an Atlas to a world map and spread it out on the table. Alongside the map, he placed a smaller book with old crumpled pages. I looked at the page it was open to. The large font at the top said "Locating Spell." He arranged four blue candles in a diamond on the table, explaining that each candle represented a point of the compass. Then he handed Chelsea a chain link with a large amethyst on the end, the point facing downward.

"This is the most important object in this ritual," he told her. "You must hold it over the map when you say the spell. The crystal will harness your power and the energy of the object when you picture it in your mind.

Once it has made the connection, it will show you on the map where the object is located."

"There's only one problem," Chelsea said. "I don't know what this ring looks like."

"This is no problem at all," Alistair said. "You and Lizzie will just have to hold hands during the spell to connect with each other. She will focus on the ring, and you will focus on harnessing the power to locate it."

I didn't particularly feel like holding hands with the girl who had cast a curse to kill me—even though we used to be best friends—but I would do it if it was the only way to locate the ring.

Chelsea held the chain with the amethyst on the end—which Alistair told us was called a pendulum—in her right hand so it hovered above the map. I grabbed her left. Alistair lit the candles, and the scent of blueberries filled the air. Drew didn't have a part in the spell, but he was still sitting in the seat next to me, watching us.

"Are you ready?" Alistair asked.

Chelsea and I nodded.

"Chelsea needs to say the spell and focus on locating the object, while Lizzie pictures it in her mind," Alistair instructed. "Picture it as clearly as possible, and recall any memories you associate with it."

I clearly remembered the gold band with the garnets around the top, and flashed back to the memories I had of my past life when Drew gave it to me.

We were outside, next to the big tree on the field behind my house that I oftentimes went to read or draw. It was close enough to the house that it wasn't a long walk, but far enough so the other trees blocked any views my mother might have had from the windows. She knew not to bother me when I went there. It was where I went when I needed time to myself.

Which made it the perfect place for Drew to meet me behind our parents' backs.

It was the day of a huge ball at the Givens' estate, and Drew's parents were insisting he spend most of the night dancing with Catherine. Even though it was only for appearance's sake, I felt jealous. Catherine and I had been close friends since we were young, and I hated how Drew's family thought she was acceptable for him to marry, and not me. It wasn't fair that just because Catherine's family had a fancy title associated with their name, it made her "appropriate" to marry. She had done nothing to deserve it. On top of everything, my parents refused to allow me to break my engagement with James—Jeremy's past self—because I couldn't tell them about my relationship with Drew until he broke things off with Catherine.

I had planned to end it with Drew that day. I couldn't imagine pushing aside the love I felt for him, but I couldn't continue to live like that, knowing his family was encouraging the courtship with Catherine and that he was taking so long to do something about it.

I was even starting to question how much he loved me.

But when he took the ring out of his pocket and placed it on my finger, telling me he had ended things with Catherine before coming over, and that the ring was a promise of his devotion to me, I knew everything was going to be okay. I trusted our love. The ring represented how far he would go—even if it meant disappointing his family—to be with me. It was everything I wanted.

It was the happiest moment of my past life.

It was also the last day I would ever see, because the carriage accident that had caused my death happened that night.

"The pendulum is moving," Chelsea said, jerking me out of my memories of the past.

"Which means the crystal has located the object." Alistair brought his hands together in excitement. "Watch it closely—it's swinging toward the spot on the map where you will find the ring."

When Chelsea started the spell, she held the crystal an inch above where we lived in Pembrooke, New Hampshire. The pendulum now swung East, and Chelsea went along with the motion, allowing the crystal to travel across the Atlantic Ocean.

When the crystal was above England, it settled down.

"Is that it?" Drew asked.

"No," Alistair replied. "It has determined the country. England. Now we need to get more specific." He reached for the Atlas and lifted the pages, scanning the table of contents. He must have found what he was looking for, because he flipped through the pages, stopping at a map of England.

The crystal started swinging again, toward the Southern part of the map. It eventually settled above Hampshire County.

The same place where Drew, Chelsea, and I lived in our past lives.

"So the ring is in Hampshire," Chelsea said. "What do we do now?"

"Simple," Alistair replied. "You go there and get it."

CHAPTER 16

"We can't just pick up and go to Hampshire," I said the first thought that popped into my mind.

"Why not?" Drew asked.

I ran my hands through my hair in frustration. "A million reasons! First of all, we have school, and we can't skip. Also, I don't have enough money to buy a flight to England without asking my mom for help. And if I did ask her for help, I doubt she would be okay with going on a random trip to England." I looked down at the map in defeat. "At least not in the next month. There's no way I can get to the ring in time."

"You're not thinking this through," Drew said patiently.

"Really?" I said, unable to believe how calm he was being. "It doesn't seem like there's much to 'think through.' But if you have a plan, then please, feel free to share. Because this is looking pretty hopeless."

"I've mentioned before that my grandparents live in England," Drew started.

"Oh, right." Chelsea rolled her eyes. "The ones who conveniently decided to visit over Halloween and made it so you had to ditch me on the night of the dance."

Drew looked at her in annoyance. "I didn't make that up—they did visit that weekend." Then he turned back to me. "More specifically, my grandparents live right outside of Southhampton. Which is in Hampshire County."

"That's great," I said. "But I don't see how that's going to get us there in time, or convince my mom to let me go at all."

"If you let me continue, I'll explain."

"All right." I waited, hoping his plan was feasible.

"Christmas is my grandparents' favorite holiday," he said. "They love celebrating it with the family, and my mom mentioned that we might visit them over winter break."

"So *you* can get there in time," I said. "What about me? I don't want to sit back and hope you're doing everything right. Not that I don't trust you to do this, but it's my future on the line. I want to help."

"And I would love for you to accompany me," Drew said. "We're leaving the day after break begins, so we'll have a week before the full moon to fix this mess. Then we can spend Christmas together, and you'll be able to see England. You'll love it there."

When he put it that way—and when I stopped thinking about Death chasing me for a few seconds—the trip did sound romantic.

"I would love to go," I told him, charmed that he had invited me. "But I'm not sure how comfortable my mom would be with my going to England with you and your mom. We haven't even been officially together for a month, and our parents haven't met yet."

"Then your mom can come too." His eyes brightened with excitement. "What better way for our moms to meet than by enjoying Christmas together in England?"

"This is all great," Chelsea said. "But you're forgetting something important."

"What's that?" I asked.

"You need me there too, since you can't get the ring to work without my borrowed magic powers helping."

"Right." And with that, my hope that this could work deflated.

"We could invite Chelsea and her dad to come along," Drew suggested. "Since your parents are dating, it would make sense to include them."

"I don't know how things work in New York City," I said, "But in Pembrooke, it's not normal to jet off to England without a month's notice. There's no way our parents will go for it."

"I might be able to help with that," Alistair said, a plan forming behind his eyes.

"How so?" I asked.

"From listening to the three of you, it sounds like the only reason why this plan would fail is because your parents are unwilling to allow you to go to England with Drew."

"Yeah," I said. "But it's a big problem. If our parents don't let us go, then we're stuck here, and we can't get the ring in time. Without the ring, we'll have no chance to fix everything. If we can't fix everything, then ..." I couldn't bring myself to say what would happen if fate continued on its current path.

"And if your parents agree to let you go, then you can locate the ring in England," Alistair continued, as if what I had said was insignificant. "This isn't a problem. With Chelsea's help, I can create a potion that will make your parents' minds more open to allowing you to go on this trip."

"Like a recipe to get them to go along with the plan?" I asked. "What are we supposed to do with it—dump it in their drinks?"

"Precisely." Alistair apparently didn't notice my skepticism. Or else he was trying to ignore it.

"I'm in," Chelsea said. "Just tell me what to do."

CHAPTER 17

An hour later, the three of us were driving home from the mall, Chelsea and I each with a vial of clear potion in our hands. I played with the vial, not liking what I was supposed to do with it tonight. I had to put it in my mom's drink before bringing up the England trip, to make her agreeable to the idea.

It felt like cheating. I didn't want to take advantage of her emotions like that.

On the other hand, it was easier than telling her about being reincarnated, Chelsea's curse, and Death coming after me. If I told her that, I had a feeling that instead of a trip to England, she would take me straight to the nearest mental institution.

"I hate that I have to do this," I said, not taking my eyes off the vial in my hands.

"You know it's the best way," Drew said. "It's either use the potion to get your mom to agree, or go behind her back."

"I know," I said. "But that doesn't mean I have to like either option."

"You're definitely going to use it, right?" Chelsea asked. "You're not going to chicken out?"

"I won't chicken out," I said, my voice firm. "Besides, I don't have much of a choice. There's no way my mom would be okay with this plan otherwise. I have to use it."

Drew pulled into Chelsea's driveway to drop her off, and I realized—too late—that it might look suspicious for us to come back from shopping without any bags. We must have gotten so involved with the plan of getting to England that we forgot about how our parents assumed we were at the mall for the Black Friday deals.

"I'll text you after I talk to my dad to let you know what he said," Chelsea told me as she got out of the car.

"All right," I said. "And remember not to let him talk to my mom until I've confirmed that we can go, too."

"Of course," Chelsea said. "Talk to you soon." She shut the door and hurried into her house.

"She's certainly gotten more agreeable," Drew said once she got inside.

"She's not that bad most of the time," I told him. "It's hard to tell from the way she's been acting recently, but there is a reason why we were friends for so long."

"She cast a curse for you to die," Drew said. Anger flared in his eyes, and he tightened his grip on the steering wheel. "And it's going to work if we don't do something about it."

"We're going to fix this," I said with more confidence than I felt. "She didn't know what she was doing when she cast that spell. If she knew she was sending Death after me, there's no way she would have done it."

"You think so?" He sounded doubtful.

"I know so," I said. "She's upset that you dumped her for me, but she's not evil. She doesn't want me dead. It's why she's helping us now."

"None of that makes it so I'm not angry about what she did."

"I'm trying not to think too much about that until we have this sorted out," I said, refocusing on the vial of clear potion in my hand. "I just hope this works and gets my mom to agree to go to England."

Drew lifted a hand from the wheel and interlaced his fingers with mine. "It will work," he said confidently. "And if it doesn't, you're coming to England with me no matter what. I'll buy you the plane ticket myself. We're going to get that ring, and then we're going to fix what Chelsea did. Your mom will be angry with you for going behind her back, but at least you'll be alive. That's all that matters to me."

I nodded, knowing he meant it. If this potion didn't make my mom more agreeable to the trip, I would have to go without her permission. I didn't want to do that— I've never gone against my mom in such an extreme way—but I wouldn't have a choice. If I didn't get to England and find that ring, I wouldn't live to see the next full moon.

Hopefully the potion would do the trick.

"Call me once you get an answer from your mom," Drew said as he pulled up to my house.

"I will," I said.

"I love you, Elizabeth," he said, his eyes locked with mine. "No matter what, we will find a way to get out of this. We just found each other again, and I don't plan on losing you anytime soon."

"I love you, too," I said, tears forming in my eyes. "Always and forever."

"We will have that," Drew promised. "Once we manage to fix this."

CHAPTER 18

Walking inside, I was painfully aware of the vial of potion in my bag and what I had to do with it in the next few minutes. At least Alistair had promised the solution was tasteless, so my mom wouldn't know I'd added it to her drink.

"Did you have fun at the mall?" my mom asked from her study.

"It was fun," I said. "Crowded, though. I'm exhausted. I'm going to make some tea—do you want some?"

"Sure," she replied. "I just have to finish something up, and then I'll be right over."

I figured that's what would happen. My mom thought Black Friday was a pseudo-holiday—a reason to get Americans shopping—so she didn't consider it an appropriate reason to take off work. I figured she was in her office dealing with paperwork, or whatever she did when I was at school.

I went into the kitchen and took out my favorite mug with the word "cocoa" written all over it in different colors, along with a plain, white mug for my mom. That way I wouldn't mix up who had which mug. I filled them up with water from the instant hot, and dropped in the teabags.

Now for the hard part.

I took out the vial and stared at the clear liquid. Drugging my mom felt so wrong. Could I go through with this? Just thinking about it made me feel like a terrible person.

Then I reminded myself that as much as I hated it, using the potion was my best option. If my mom didn't agree to the plan, then I either had to go to England behind her back, or be doomed to die by the next full moon.

The idea that I could die was frightening. Hadn't I faced enough imminent death by keeping Jeremy from getting us in a deadly car accident last weekend? I never thought that at sixteen I would be worrying about dying. Yet here I was, knowing that because of one selfish act from someone who I once considered my best friend, I might not live to see my seventeenth birthday. The whole situation made me feel helpless and out of control.

I uncapped the vial, and dumped the potion into my mom's drink.

As much as I told myself that I was doing what I had to, it didn't make me feel any better.

"What did you get at the mall?" my mom asked as she entered the kitchen.

"I couldn't find anything," I said. "It was crowded, and the lines were so long for the dressing rooms and to purchase anything that I didn't feel like waiting. I'm never going to the mall on Black Friday again."

"I guess that's a lesson you have to learn the hard way," my mom said with a laugh. "It's why I do my Black Friday shopping online."

Apparently she was getting some shopping in while claiming to work.

"Yeah," I agreed. I took a sip of my tea, and then handed my mom her mug.

"This is good," she said. "What kind of tea did you use?"

"It's just cinnamon," I said, feeling guilty about the lie. I hoped the strong flavor of cinnamon would cover up any possible taste of the potion, despite the fact that it was supposed to be tasteless.

"I'm glad you and Chelsea are friends again," my mom said, taking a seat at the table. "I had a feeling the two of you would work it out."

I joined her at the table. She'd taken a few sips of tea, so the potion was in her system.

It was now or never.

"When the three of us were at the mall, Drew invited us to spend Christmas with him," I said nervously. My mom's mind was supposed to be "relaxing and opening to new possibilities," but I dreaded she would immediately say no when I brought up the trip.

"Do you mean you, Drew, and Chelsea?" my mom asked suspiciously. I couldn't blame her for thinking the offer was strange. It would make sense if he invited me, but she knew there was bad history between the three of us.

"It's a family thing, so he invited our families as well. He figured it would be nice to invite Chelsea and her dad since the two of you are dating."

"That was thoughtful of him," my mom said. "Will it be at his house?"

"That's the thing." I dreaded the next words that were going to come out of my mouth. "They're spending Christmas with his grandparents in England."

My mom nearly choked on her tea. "So you're saying he invited us to England?"

"Yes." I tried to remain calm and not worry about her minor freak out. Maybe she needed time to let it soak in. "His grandparents' house is large enough to host all of us, so we won't have to stay in a hotel. All we would need are the plane flights."

She took another sip of tea, and I could tell she was considering it. A spark of hope passed through my chest. She hadn't said an immediate no, which was what I had feared.

Maybe she would actually go for this plan.

"I do have airline miles set aside that need to be used," she said.

"So we can go?"

"I'll check the flights, and if I'm able to use the miles to get free airfare, then we can go. I've always wanted to spend Christmas somewhere exotic. It might be a nice change."

"Wow," I said, surprised by how easy that was. Not like I should have been surprised—I gave her a big nudge with the potion. "Can you check the flights now?" I wanted to make sure she purchased them before the potion wore off.

"First, why don't you ask Drew for his flight information so I can try booking the same one?" She didn't even sound skeptical. If anything, she sounded excited. This was more than I had hoped for.

I took out my cell and texted him.

I'm sitting with my mom right now so I can't call, but she seems on board with the plan! She wants to know your flight information so we can try to get on the same one.

A minute later, he texted me the information. I relayed it to my mom.

"Come with me to the study and I'll check the flights," she said.

I couldn't believe she was agreeing so easily. Actually I could believe it, since I gave her the potion, but I didn't really think it would work.

I also wondered if she would have agreed if I hadn't used it at all. Maybe she would have. I doubted she would have said yes so fast, but I liked to think she wouldn't have been completely opposed to the idea.

I felt bad that I had to manipulate her with the potion, but at the same time, I was going to ENGLAND! I'd wanted to go to England for years. My fascination with the country probably had to do with how I'd lived a past life there. And now I was finally getting a chance to visit! It was like something out of a dream.

For a moment, I was so excited about going to England that I forgot the reasons behind the trip. If we didn't go, find the ring, and stop my death in the past, this might be the last vacation I took in my life.

"It looks like my miles work for these flights," my mom said as she typed the information into the places necessary to get the round trip flights. "And now we're officially going to England for Christmas vacation!" she said with a final click of the mouse.

She just got the tickets—we're going to England! I texted Drew.

"Who are you texting?" she asked.

If there was one question that always annoyed me, it was when my mom asked who I was texting. But I answered anyway, unable to hide my smile when I said Drew's name. "Just telling him that we're officially in for the trip," I explained.

"Any news from Chelsea?" my mom asked. "Tyler doesn't like flying. I should have asked him before booking the flights ... it's strange I didn't think of that first." Her forehead creased, and I could tell she was genuinely confused. Which made me feel guilty, since she definitely would have asked him first if it hadn't been for the potion in her tea making her do what I asked.

"I'll ask Chelsea," I said.

I texted Chelsea to ask about her progress, hoping her response would be positive. If Chelsea couldn't come, then the plan wouldn't work. We needed her temporary affinity with magic to accomplish what was necessary.

Her reply arrived less than a minute later.

My dad hates flying, but he's almost there. Are you definitely going? If you are, that would help him make up his mind.

YES! I replied. *My mom just got the tickets!*

"Chelsea said it seems like her dad is going to say yes," I told my mom, since she was waiting for me to relay what the text said.

"I don't understand why you can't call each other," she said with a shake of her head. "It's much faster than texting."

I laughed, because as many times as I tried to explain texting to my mom, she never got it. I called people if I needed to have a long conversation, but for anything else, texting was more efficient.

But I didn't say that to my mom, because I'd told her a million times and it never sunk in.

My phone buzzed with another text from Chelsea.

My dad is IN!

"Chelsea and her dad are coming on the trip!" I told my mom. Right away, I texted Drew to let him know.

I couldn't believe this was coming together so easily.

CHAPTER 19

I'd never traveled internationally before, so I didn't know what to expect. The plane was huge—much larger than the planes I took when I visited my dad in Pennsylvania. My mom, Chelsea, Chelsea's dad, and I had seats near each other in coach. Drew and his mom were in first class. The leather seats in first class looked big and comfortable, but I tried not to be jealous. We were all ending up in the same place. Plus, the coach seats had little touch screen televisions, so I could stay entertained through the flight.

We were supposed to sleep since we were traveling East, but I couldn't fall asleep on planes, so I read the whole way. The lack of sleep would catch up with me tomorrow, but there was no point in uncomfortably trying (and failing) to sleep when I could read instead.

It was morning in England when we arrived. To me, it felt like night should have just started. I regretted not sleeping on the plane, since I was getting the feeling that the jet lag was going to be rough.

When we got to baggage claim at Heathrow Airport, I saw a middle-aged man in a suit holding a sign that said "Carmichael." He waved when he spotted Drew and Drew's mom.

"That's my grandparents' driver, Marshall," Drew told me. "My grandparents are doing last minute preparations for our arrival, so they'll be meeting us at the house."

I looked at him in amazement. "Your grandparents have a driver?"

"Yeah." He squeezed my hand for assurance. I guess he didn't realize how alien the concept of having a personal driver would seem to me until he saw my reaction. Maybe drivers were commonplace in London and New York City, but in Pembrooke, everyone I knew drove themselves.

Marshall helped us with our luggage, and led us out of the airport to a huge limo.

"And they have a limo?" I asked Drew, keeping my voice quiet. I didn't want Marshall to overhear me and think I was unsophisticated.

"Yep," he said. "But they only use it to go to important functions, or to the airport."

"And to go to other places they use what ... their Rolls Royce?" I was only half-joking.

"Close," Drew said. "They have a Bentley."

I didn't know much about Bentleys, but I guessed they were expensive.

"The drive will take about an hour and fifteen minutes," Marshall told us once he finished loading our luggage into the limo.

The limo was huge, and the wraparound seat provided more than enough room for the six of us. Drew and his mom sat in the forward-facing seat, Chelsea and her dad took the seat facing backward, and my mom and I sat in the longest seat that faced the side. I liked that, because the window was straight ahead, giving me a good view of the scenery.

Everyone made small talk on the way there, but I spaced out of the conversation to admire the view. When we first left the airport the surroundings were urban, although the city had a historical feel to it, since the buildings had been there for centuries. It was incredible thinking about everything that might have happened in those buildings for the hundreds of years that they've been there. So many families that have come and gone, so many stories to tell.

The sidewalks were covered in snow, but the grayness of winter couldn't take away the charmed feeling I got while looking around. I spotted a few of the British red telephone booths that I'd seen in movies, and as we drove farther from the city we passed the cutest houses that looked like they'd been in families for generations. Everything felt classy here—even the taxicabs were black and regal, opposed to the dinky, yellow ones in the United States. Hopefully I would have time later in the trip to sketch some of these beautiful scenes.

The buildings grew farther apart as the drive continued, and I admired the rolling hills of the English countryside. The snow blanketed on the grass and trees made it look like we were in a winter wonderland. Not even the gray sky distracted from the mystical feeling, and goose bumps rose across my arms as I contemplated the years of history held within these enchanting lands.

I couldn't believe I was here—in England—the place where a past self I was only beginning to remember had lived out the entirety of her life that had been cut off too soon.

Which reminded me that if Drew, Chelsea, and I weren't successful on our mission, my present life might be cut off soon, too.

With that thought, the sky that had been welcoming only minutes before took on a foreboding quality. I wrapped my arms around myself and sunk into the seat, not wanting to think about the dire consequences that would happen if the task Alistair had set for us turned out to be impossible. I wanted to be optimistic, but it was hard when what we had to do was so extreme.

Finally, Marshall pulled up in front of a huge house that I assumed belonged to Drew's grandparents. Actually, "house" was barely a fair description. The only proper term I could come up with for it was an estate.

The Tudor-style home was three floors tall, with huge windows on the stone walls and a double-door entrance that looked too heavy for one person alone to open. I knew that Drew came from a wealthy family, but I had no idea his grandparents lived in a place fit for nobility. Along with the house being huge, there were no other houses nearby, giving me the impression that Drew's grandparents owned most of the surrounding land. I couldn't imagine how two people could need that much space for themselves.

I wondered if it ever got lonely. That must be why they opened their home for guests, like they were doing for my and Chelsea's families now. Single lights in each window were the only signs that the house was prepared for the holiday season, and I could make out a giant Christmas tree in one of the larger windows near the door.

This was going to be the most magical Christmas ever.

And hopefully it wouldn't be my last.

I stepped out of the limo, and Drew held out a hand to help me up.

"What do you think?" he asked. "Is England how you pictured it?"

"This house looks like it's for nobility!" I blurted, embarrassed after I said it. I didn't want to sound like a hick from the middle of nowhere in New Hampshire, but I couldn't contain my enthusiasm.

"My grandparents don't have noble titles," Drew said with a laugh.

"I didn't think so," I said.

"Because my grandfather was the third son," Drew continued, "so his eldest brother got the title."

My mouth must have dropped open, because Drew chuckled and pulled me closer. I hadn't prepared to meet a noble British family! I looked at what I was wearing—jeans, UGG boots, and a white puffy jacket.

His grandparents were going to think I was totally pedestrian.

"Don't worry," Drew said, as if he could read my mind. "They're going to love you."

"How do you know?" I asked.

"Because I love you," he said, nuzzling his nose into my cheek. "So they have no other choice but to love you as well."

Despite the freezing air, his words sent warmth shooting through my body.

"Come on," he said, draping an arm around my shoulders. "Let's go inside and meet them."

"Shouldn't we get our bags first?" I asked. I wanted to go into the warmness of the house, but I didn't want to leave my bags in the limo. I supposed Marshall might bring them inside, but it seemed rude to assume so.

"You're a guest here," Drew said. "Your luggage will be taken care of and brought to your room. Now, do you want to walk inside, or are you going to make me carry you there myself?"

"Let's go," I said, despite the temptation of Drew's offer. I would have loved for him to carry me inside, but it was too soon for Chelsea to see us being so affectionate around each other.

He squeezed my hand, and we walked toward the massive front doors.

CHAPTER 20

Drew's grandparents were waiting for us inside the living room. They introduced themselves by their first names, Richard and Sara. After the introductions, they offered us tea—it was so British. Then again, we were in England, and they were British, so it made sense.

The antique furniture made me feel like I was in a museum, and I sat down gently on the velvet couch as to not hurt it. Which was silly, since it had survived all those years, but I'd never been in a home this extravagant. Not even Drew's compared.

"We're glad you were able to make it," Drew's grandma said to me warmly. She reminded me of a queen—slender, and dressed in an ivory dress suit and pearls. "Drew's told us so much about you, and it's lovely that you'll be spending Christmas with us."

"Thank you for inviting us," I replied. "And for having us stay with you. Your home is beautiful."

"We need a reason to fill up these guest rooms," Drew's grandpa said with a hearty laugh. "Don't get me wrong—I love living out here—but country life does get rather quiet."

We talked for about twenty more minutes—mainly Drew's grandparents asking Drew, Chelsea, and me about school and New Hampshire. Then the jet lag caught up with me. As hard as I tried, I couldn't stop from yawning. I felt bad, since we had only just arrived. I didn't want Drew's grandparents to think they were boring me, but I felt like I hadn't slept in over a day.

"Did you get much sleep on the plane, dear?" Drew's grandma asked, placing her teacup down on the saucer.

"Not really," I managed in between yawns.

"Lizzie didn't sleep at all on the plane," my mom decided to speak on my behalf. "She read the entire time."

"You didn't sleep at all?" Chelsea's dad looked horrified.

"I tried, but it was hard to sleep in the seats," I said with a shrug. I didn't look at Drew or his mom, since I'm sure it was easier for them to sleep in the cushy first class seats that leaned back into private beds. I didn't want to be jealous, but I kind of was, a little.

I shouldn't be thinking that way, though, since I was lucky to be here at all.

"Perhaps you want to rest up before dinner?" Drew's grandma asked. Then she looked around at everyone else, and I noticed that I wasn't the only one with dark circles under my eyes. My mom tried to stifle a yawn, but I could tell she was tired as well.

"It seems like you all need a good nap," Drew's grandma concluded. "I'll show you to your rooms—I know how tough travel days can be, so the staff has already prepared them for you."

I was so tired that I didn't show as much surprise as I normally would have at the fact that they had an entire staff. I was like a zombie as I followed her down the hall.

First she led Chelsea and her dad to their room, and the next one was for me and my mom. It was bigger than the master bedroom at our house, and the traditional furniture looked fit for nobility.

I didn't have much time to admire it, because the moment I got into the bed, I closed my eyes and instantly fell asleep.

* * *

When the alarm on my phone sounded to wake me for dinner, I could have sworn it was the next day already and I had accidentally slept through the night. I needed ten more hours of sleep if I would ever feel awake again. But Drew's grandparents had mentioned at tea that they were having dinner prepared for us to welcome us to England. As much as I would have loved to have slept through until morning, I forced myself to get out of bed and change out of the travel clothes I'd been wearing since I got on the plane in New Hampshire, which was who knows how long ago.

Dinner was served in the formal dining room, and it was extremely elegant. I felt like a lady in Downton Abbey, one of my favorite television shoes. Also, Drew's grandma had no part in preparing the meal—besides deciding what she wanted on the menu. They actually did have a full staff, so their personal chef, Zesa, made our food. When each course was served, she told us details about the dish. I would have been more than happy with a cheeseburger and fries, but the Beef Wellington we had as an entrée was delicious. I barely had room for dessert, but I managed to force some cake down to be polite.

"Are you more awake after your nap?" Drew asked once the meal was over.

"Sort of," I said, rubbing my eyes and holding back a yawn. "I'd heard about jet lag, but I never knew it was like this. I've never felt so tired before."

"If you can manage to stay up for a little longer, I would love to give you a tour of the gardens," he said.

"At night?" I asked. "And in December?" Just thinking about it made me shiver.

"Winter gardens have a certain charm to them," he said. "And while they're beautiful during the day, I prefer them at night."

I wasn't surprised. Drew was more of a night owl than me.

"I might be able to force myself to stay awake for a little bit longer," I said with a smile.

He squeezed my hand. "Glad to hear it."

After thanking Drew's grandparents and Chef Zesa for the meal, Drew and I bundled up in winter gear and headed out to the gardens. I was worried that Chelsea would try to come with us, but either she got the hint that we wanted to be by ourselves or she was extremely tired, because she said she was exhausted and went to bed.

I wished I felt more awake, but this was the first chance I had to be alone with Drew since arriving to England. I was at least going to pretend to not be tired.

The garden was huge, and unbelievably beautiful. It had stone walls around it, and to enter we walked through an archway that looked like it led to another world. It was so quiet that even the sounds of our feet on stray twigs sounded loud. We strolled along the cobblestone pathway, and I was enjoying myself despite the cold, which was saying a lot. But English winters weren't as bad as the ones in New Hampshire, so it was bearable.

I didn't say much as I took in the view. All the trees except the evergreens were bare and covered in snow. White Christmas lights wrapped around the occasional tree, transforming the garden into a winter wonderland. Carved stone pots looked like they would hold flowers in the summer, but in the winter, with icicles dripping down the handles, they had a charm of their own. Once more, I wished for my sketchbook.

"It's beautiful," I said, leaning closer into Drew as we walked. I loved being near him, and the proximity kept me warm.

"I like gardens best in the winter," he said.

"Why?" I asked.

"Because that's when the garden is in its purest form," he said. "Sure, it's more colorful in the summer, but in the winter you see the bare bones of what it is, of what keeps it alive."

Looking around now, what he said made sense. I would have loved to see what the garden looked like in the summer, in complete bloom, but now I was seeing the heart of what made it up, the part that never died.

Then I glanced up at the sky and saw the moon. It was three-quarters full. It would have been beautiful, but instead it reminded me that I only had a week to fix what Chelsea had done.

Drew must have seen the worry etched on my face, because he pulled me closer. I rested my head on his shoulder, loving being near him. I wished we could stay like this forever—the two of us together, enjoying a nighttime walk through a garden in the middle of winter. If only we didn't have so much to worry about. Then we could be happy, like we were meant to be.

"Want to sit?" he asked when we came across a wooden bench. It had a covering above it, so the seat wasn't wet with snow. The wood was old and peeling, making the bench look like it belonged in a cottage instead of a semi-noble estate. "This is my favorite place in the garden."

He put his arm around me when we sat down, and I snuggled into him, breathing in the coldness of winter tinged with his forest-y cologne. For the rest of my life, I would associate the scent of the forest with safety, happiness, and love.

We looked up at the moon and stars, my hand clasped in his, neither of us saying a word.

"I can't believe everything Alistair wants us to do," I voiced what had been on my mind since speaking with him at his store. "It feels so impossible."

"I wish I could tell you something that would make it all okay, or help prepare us for what's to come, but I have no idea about this time travel stuff, either," Drew said. "I want it to work, but whenever I think about it, it sounds crazy, and like you said, impossible. It's our only option, though, so we have to try."

"We can't lose anything by trying."

"Exactly." He nodded. "And we'll lose everything if we don't."

"Every time I think about it, it makes my head spin," I told him.

"How come?" he asked.

"For instance, let's say it's possible, and the time travel works," I started. "In the timeline we have now, we never went back to the past. Everything that exists in this life happened *because* of what happened in the past. Us meeting again, stopping the accident so we could be together in this life, etcetera. If we go back to the past and change it … what if we come back and everything is different? We could be completely different people. And if everything changes, will we remember everything from this timeline—the life we've lived up until now—or from the new one we'll create by going back to the past?"

Drew took a minute to process everything I'd said. I couldn't blame him, since it was all rather confusing.

"You're getting ahead of yourself," he finally decided. "There's no point in worrying about things like that. Because this time line—what's going to happen if we can't go back and change everything—ends in Chelsea's spell taking hold of you, and you know how that will end. If we can change anything, it has to be better than what's going to happen if we don't."

"You're right," I said. "I just hope we don't cause a major paradox."

"Did you watch some crazy sci-fi movie on the plane?" Drew asked with a laugh.

"Not on the plane." I laughed too, even though I was stressed out. "But I've watched them before, and seen TV shows about it and read books about it. The moment time travel gets involved in a story, everything gets confusing. The smallest change in the past can have huge effects on the future."

Drew tucked a curl behind my ear. "You can't think about it like that," he said, serious now. "This is the only chance we have to fix things. Whatever happens once we've finished, it has to be better than what we're facing now."

He kissed me then, sweet and loving, the warmth of his lips making the cold disappear around me. In moments like this, it was only me and Drew, and nothing could touch us.

If only those moments could last forever.

CHAPTER 21

After breakfast the next morning, Drew, Chelsea, and I met in Drew's room to start our search. Just like at Alistair's, we set up a map of the area, and Chelsea held the pendulum as I pictured the ring. But as hard as we tried, we couldn't get it to work. It was like the balance of power was off.

After multiple tries, we admitted defeat.

"Without the tracking spell, how are we supposed to find one ring in the entire county?" Chelsea had no problem pointing out the grim reality of our situation. "It'll be like trying to find a needle in a haystack."

When she said it like that, it did sound extremely grim.

"I've already thought about this," Drew said confidently. "You know how Lizzie has Alistair in New Hampshire, and he's her Memory Guide?"

"Yeah ..." Chelsea nodded, looking doubtful about whatever he was about to say.

"Well, I have a Memory Guide here in Hampshire County. She's the one who helped me remember my past life on that trip to England two years ago. Her name is Misty, and she has a shop in town."

"So we can visit her and figure out where to go from here," I concluded what Drew must have been thinking.

"You got it," he said with a knowing smile.

It was decided, then. Drew told his grandparents that he was going to show us around town, they called in the driver for us, and we were off.

* * *

The town he was referring to was called Winchester, and it was the most charming place I had ever seen. We passed so many beautiful buildings on the drive—a huge cathedral, a castle, and other historic sites that I wanted to run inside of and explore. But we were on a mission, and that mission unfortunately did not include site-seeing like a tourist.

Marshall dropped us off, and Drew led Chelsea and me down a pedestrian-only street called Winchester High Street. No building was taller than three floors, and each one had an individual antique front. I felt like I was on a set for a historical movie. There were flower boxes in lots of the windows, and I imagined they would have been beautiful in the summer.

We walked down the stone walkway until we reached a wrought iron clock jutting out of one of the buildings. Across from the clock was a shop with a Tudor-front and thatched roof, the hanging sign reading "Misty's Antiques."

"Good, she's still here," Drew said.

"You didn't know if she was still here?" Chelsea rolled her eyes. "What would you have done if she wasn't?"

"Worried about it then?" Drew said nonchalantly.

"Good to know you've got this under control," Chelsea shot back. "So glad to be trusting you with something so important."

"It doesn't matter, because she *is* here," I said. If Chelsea and Drew kept picking on each other, I was going to get annoyed fast. "Let's go in and say hi."

We walked into the store, and the bell on the door jingled to announce our arrival.

The shop had a similar feeling to Alistair's—small and dark, with antiques pushed together in every possible space. I could spend a long time searching through everything to discover something truly special. The store was a lot busier than Alistair's, though, with what looked like tourists and locals alike browsing the items and chatting with each other.

Misty was in the back, ringing up items for a customer. Because of Alistair, I expected her to be old and mysterious—the stereotype antique owner. But she was nothing like that. She was young—maybe in her upper twenties or lower thirties—her brown hair styled in trendy curls and wearing a lacy green dress that looked like it came from a designer store. If I had seen her on the street, I would have thought she worked at a fashion magazine, not a musty antique shop.

"Is that her?" Chelsea sounded as surprised as I felt.

"Yep," Drew said.

"I expected someone more like Alistair," I said. "She looks cool."

"She *is* cool," Drew replied. "Did you think my Memory Guide would be anything but?"

I laughed, glad that Drew could joke around despite everything we were dealing with. Of course now that I thought about our situation, the weight of it came pouring over me, but it was nice to have those few seconds when my imminent death wasn't consuming my every thought.

"Drew Carmichael." Misty smiled as we approached, and had a younger employee she called Lauren take over at the register. "And I'm guessing you're Elizabeth?"

"Yes." I wasn't surprised she knew who I was—Alistair had known who Drew was without me introducing them, too. It must be a Memory Guide thing.

"And you are?" Misty looked at Chelsea, confusion on her made-up face.

"Chelsea Givens," Chelsea introduced herself. "I love your dress."

"Thanks!" Misty smiled, and it was like the two of them were friends already.

"Sorry to come by when it's so busy," Drew said. "But we need to talk to you about something important."

"No worries," Misty said with a wave of her hand. "I have a bunch of holiday workers who would love to help out. I'll let them know, then we can get tea nearby and chat."

"This isn't the sort of conversation we can have in public," I whispered to Drew.

He repeated what I'd said to Misty.

She nodded, and after letting Lauren know what was going on, led us to a back room that I guessed was her office, although it was so messy it was hard to tell.

We sat down on the couches and chairs, and caught her up on everything until now.

"Do you think what Alistair wants us to do is possible?" I asked once we finished telling her the story.

"I've heard rumors of such things, but I've never witnessed it myself," she said. "Everything in the Universe must line up perfectly, and it's rare when that happens. But we'll never know if we don't try, right?"

She was so optimistic that it was hard to disagree.

"Do you have an idea how to help us find the ring?" Drew asked.

"I was wondering when you would ask," Misty said, a smile on her glossed lips. "The tracking spell didn't work earlier because there were only three of you in the room. It's easiest with four, since it relates to the four directions of the compass—North, South, East, and West. Now that the three of you are here with me, we'll be able to do the tracking spell with much more accuracy."

"It's also more accurate when the person doing the spell is closer to the object, right?" I asked.

"Correct," she said. "When you were in America, you were able to narrow the location of the ring down to

Hampshire County. Now that you're here, and your energy is closer to the ring, the connection will be enormously stronger. We should be able to get it to an exact location."

"What are we waiting for, then?" Chelsea said. "Let's get started."

CHAPTER 22

It didn't take long for us to pinpoint the location of the ring.

"Where is that?" I asked, looking at the spot on the map. The location felt familiar. Almost like I knew where it was, although I had never been there before.

"It appears to be a residential address," Misty said. "If we want to find the ring, we'll have to go inside."

"Like breaking and entering?" I couldn't believe she was proposing such a thing.

"Nothing so incriminating, no." Misty looked deep in thought. "We'll figure something out. But first, we have to go there and scout out what we're dealing with. Once we get more information, we'll come up with a plan."

I didn't like the sound of that, but I didn't have any better ideas, so we squished into Misty's small car and headed to our destination.

* * *

When we pulled up in front of the house, I knew why the location felt familiar.

"That's the house from my past," I said breathlessly. "The one I lived in when I was her—Elizabeth."

I remembered it clearly from when I described it without meaning to in French class earlier in the school year. Two stories tall, white wood siding, and the wraparound porch covered with ivy. The swing attached to a huge tree in front—the same swing from the memories I had with Drew when we were our past selves. It was the swing my past self sketched him sitting in when our families had no idea we were together.

I couldn't believe I was here, and that this place existed. I mean, I knew it existed, but it always felt like it existed in another life—because up until now, it had.

"You're sure the ring is in there?" I asked Misty.

"That's what the pendulum said when Chelsea did the tracking spell." She pulled the car up to the end of the driveway and put it into park.

"What do we do now?" I asked. "We can't just knock on the door and tell whoever lives there that we're searching for a garnet ring she has, because it was mine in a past life and since my best friend accidentally cursed me to die, we need the ring now because it might be able to take us back in time, where we can stop the curse from happening in the first place."

"Did you really get that out in one breath?" Misty laughed.

"And someone's probably home," I added, "Because there's a car in the driveway."

"Lizzie has a point." Chelsea looked at Drew, like he might have the answer. "What are we supposed to do from here?"

"Don't look at me," he said. "I was hoping no one would be home so we could go inside and look around. We could wait for whoever lives there to leave, but we have no idea when that might be."

"I'll have to distract them, then," Misty said, like this was no issue at all.

"And then what?" I looked at her with wide eyes. "Have us sneak in and find the ring?"

Her eyes glinted with mischief. "Precisely."

I couldn't believe she seriously suggested that. "How are we supposed to find the ring in the house?" I asked. "And what if the owner is wearing it? Then we have no chance."

"If the owner is wearing it, then I'll be able to see it, and I'll handle it," Misty said. "Now, calm down and think. Where do you think you would be most likely to find a ring?"

"A jewelry chest in the master bedroom," I said the first idea that popped into my mind. "At least that's where my mom keeps her nice pieces."

"That wasn't hard to figure out," Misty said. "So, here's the plan."

She proceeded to tell us her crazy idea that just might work.

CHAPTER 23

I couldn't believe we were going through with this. I'd only broken one rule in my life, when I'd sneaked out of my house to spend time with Drew before anyone knew we were together. Every time I did that, I felt awful knowing I wasn't being honest with my mom.

Now I was breaking and entering? It was one thing sneaking out of my house, but sneaking *into* one? One that wasn't mine? Maybe it was mine in a past life, so it wasn't as bad as it could have been, but now a complete stranger owned it. According to the law, I had no connection with this house.

This would be my first—and hopefully last—criminal act.

Drew and I were waiting in the car with Misty, since Chelsea had gone ahead to check out the situation. Misty's cell phone lit up with a text message.

"Chelsea says it's all clear," Misty whispered in her best Mission Impossible voice. "Go join her and I'll do my thing. Once I leave with the owner, do exactly what I told you."

Drew and I got out of the car and closed the door. We walked to the house, my hand staying in his the whole time.

"You're shaking," he said, giving my hand a squeeze. "Relax."

"How am I supposed to relax knowing what we're about to do?"

"If you want, you can take Chelsea's position on look-out and she can go inside the house with me to find the ring," he suggested.

"No way." I didn't have to think twice about my answer. I didn't want to be the one outside—by myself—while Chelsea was in the house with Drew. "The house layout is in my past memory, so I'm the best one to go inside with you and find the ring."

"Let's get this over with, then," he said. "It shouldn't be too hard—we'll be in and out of there in no time. Plus, this is nothing compared to what we have to do after we get the ring."

He had a point, but it wasn't making me feel any better.

Drew and I walked as quietly as possible around the house and joined Chelsea by the side.

"What did you see?" I asked her.

"It seems like there's only one person home—a lady who looks like she's our parents' age," Chelsea said. "I peeked through the windows on the first floor, and there were no bedrooms, so you were right that the master is on the second floor."

"Great," I said. Hopefully Misty was right and her self-proclaimed "gift of gab" would distract the lady who owned the house long enough for us to sneak inside and get the ring.

Now we just had to wait for her to do her thing.

I couldn't see Misty from where the three of us stood to the side of the house, but I heard her walk up to the door and knock. A few seconds later, someone answered.

"How may I help you?" a woman asked in a polite British accent.

One thing I'd noticed since arriving in England was that British people always sounded polite. They could be talking about the most vulgar thing ever and still make it sound proper.

It was hard to imagine that in my past life, I had an accent like that, too.

"I'm so glad someone's home!" Misty said, sounding flustered. "I was on my way to meet a client and my car broke down in the middle of the street! I have no idea what's wrong with it, and my cell is getting such terrible reception that I can't make an outgoing call."

"Oh, dear," the woman said, not sounding bothered at all. She introduced herself as Barbara, and from her voice, she sounded older, like the type of woman who sat inside knitting and reading all day with a bunch of cats nearby. "Would you like to come inside and borrow my phone?"

"Do you think you could take a look at the car with me?" Misty asked.

"As much as I would love to help, I'm hardly an expert with cars ..." Barbara replied.

"At least come outside with me and let me borrow your cell," Misty insisted. "You must have a different service provider than I do, and I'll want to be near the car when talking with the professionals, don't you agree? It would be much easier to tell them what's wrong."

"I suppose that makes sense," Barbara said. "Let me fetch my cell and I'll go outside with you. Wait here—I'll be back in a minute."

After Barbara got her cell, the two of them headed toward the car. I peeked around the side of the house to get a glimpse of what Barbara looked like. I could only see the back of her head, but she didn't look like I'd pictured. From this angle, I guessed she was in her forties or fifties. She was tall, with long brown hair, and she was wearing workout clothes. I supposed she wasn't expecting company.

"You have to move," Chelsea whispered to me, reminding me why we were here.

Drew led the way to the back of the house. I followed him, unable to believe I was going through with this.

Just like Chelsea had said after her initial investigation, the back door was unlocked. I supposed residents of the English countryside didn't worry about people breaking and entering when they were home.

"Good luck," Chelsea said before Drew and I went inside.

I was still upset at her about everything that had happened in the past few months, but I was glad we were sort of friends again. I hoped that given time, our relationship would return to normal.

Well, as normal as it could be given what we'd gone through.

Drew and I walked into the house, and I was struck with déjà-vu. The breakfast area looked familiar, with its wooden floors and windows looking out to the backyard. It wasn't completely as I remembered, though. The electronic objects inside, like the coffee maker, microwave, and toaster, felt out of place. Still, I could perfectly visualize what the kitchen looked like before modern conveniences existed.

"The stairs are near the front," I whispered to Drew, anxious to keep moving. As much as I would have loved to explore every nook and cranny of this house where I'd lived in a past life, we had a time constraint. I didn't know how long Misty could keep Barbara occupied with the car breaking down story, and I didn't want to test our luck.

We walked to the stairs, trying to be as quiet as possible. I was better at this than Drew. Every time a plank of wood squeaked beneath his feet, I cringed, even though Misty and Barbara were at the end of the driveway and neither of them could hear us. Still, it was nerve-wracking.

I took the lead as we walked up the steps, and I didn't need to think twice about where the master bedroom was. I just opened the door and walked inside.

But while I knew the layout of the house, that was the only thing about it that had stayed the same. Barely any of the furniture remained from when I lived there in my past life; it was like everything about that existence had disappeared.

I wondered what had happened—if my family took the furniture with them when they moved, if they sold it, or if the new owner got rid of it to make room for her belongings. The house couldn't have been kept in the family, since I was an only child, and my past self didn't live long enough to marry and have children.

What had happened to my parents back then? Did they move after the death of their only child to start life fresh, or did they die in this house at an old age, ending the family line forever?

"Is everything okay?" Drew's concerned voice brought me back to the present.

"Yeah," I said. "Being here and knowing that this is where I used to live is just a lot to take in."

"I understand," he told me. "But we have to find the ring and get out of here. Maybe we can look around at some other point, but now isn't the time."

"I know," I said, and looked around to locate the jewelry box.

It wasn't hard to find. It sat on top of an antique chest of drawers—I recognized the chest as one that had been there when my past self had lived in the house. It looked freshly painted and renovated, but it was definitely the same one.

"It's over there," I said to Drew, pointing at the wooden box that was also a relic from the past.

We walked up to it, and stared at it as though afraid to touch it.

"You can open it," he told me, watching me intensely.

I looked back at the box, unable to believe that this might hold the ring the two of us had made a promise on all those years ago, in a life we were only beginning to remember. A promise to be with each other forever ... a promise that was strong enough to transcend time.

I lifted the lid of the box and there it was, sitting in the center of the ring section. The gold band with a half-moon of garnets along the top, gleaming even in the low-lighted room.

Looking at it sent images flashing through my mind of Drew and I together on the field outside this house, when he presented it to me and told me he ended the engagement with Catherine and it was me he wanted to spend the rest of his life with. How he didn't care what his family thought, or what they would do to him out of anger. It was worth it for us to be together, because he loved me, and he would never find anyone else he wanted to be with more.

Before either of us could grab the ring, my cell phone lit up. A text from Chelsea.

911 – they're heading back to the house!

Panic pounded through my chest, and I showed Drew the text.

He grabbed the ring from the jewelry box and shoved it into the front pocket of his jeans. "Keep quiet, and maybe we can get out the back before she sees us," he whispered.

We tip-toed out of the bedroom in time to hear the front door open. I froze at the top of the steps.

"Thank you so much for your help!" Misty's voice resonated through the entire house. "I can't believe it was something so simple!"

"It was no trouble at all." I could tell from the edge in Barbara's voice that she was getting annoyed. "Is there something else you need?"

"I've got a long drive ahead, and would appreciate using the loo before heading out," Misty said. "I'm also dying of thirst—do you have any iced tea, perhaps?"

"I'll go fetch it," Barbara said, and then directed Misty to the restroom.

"This is our chance," I whispered to Drew. "We'll have to leave through the front door." I couldn't believe I sounded calm, when I was freaking out inside.

"Let's go," he said, not wasting any time before rushing down the stairwell. I followed him, cringing every time my steps were loud enough to be overheard. Luckily, the stairs led straight to the front door.

We burst outside, making sure to shut the door quietly behind us.

Once on the porch, I took a deep breath of fresh air and ran with Drew down the driveway until we reached the car. Chelsea was already there waiting for us.

"I can't believe you guys made it!" she said, breathless from what I guessed was also her dash to the car. "Did you get the ring?"

"It's right here." Drew patted the front pocket of his jeans.

"When they went inside the house, I thought for sure we were going to get caught!" I ran my hands through my hair in an attempt to tame my curls. "I can't believe we got away with it."

"What's going to happen when Barbara realizes her ring is missing?" Chelsea asked.

I hadn't considered that part, but now that Chelsea brought it up, I ran through the possibilities.

"If we don't succeed with our plan, she'll eventually realize it's gone," I said with a shrug.

"And if we do succeed with our plan?"

I met her eyes, and tried to sound more confident than I felt. "If we do succeed with our plan, then she won't notice the ring is gone, because it never would have been hers to begin with."

"What does that mean?" Chelsea looked confused.

"If everything works out the way we want, I will never have died in the past, so the path the ring took to get to this point will have changed completely," I explained. "My past self will live a long life, with the ring in her possession, and will probably pass it down through her family so it doesn't end up with a stranger like it did in this reality."

Chelsea nodded, although I could tell she was having a hard time digesting this. I could somewhat grasp it because of the books I enjoyed reading, but Chelsea never shared my interest in science-fiction and fantasy.

I didn't have more time to explain time travel theory to her, because Misty hurried down the driveway and joined us at the car.

"Did you get the ring?" she asked, her eyes wide in hope. "Please tell me you did and I didn't go through that for nothing."

"We got it," I assured her. "Although I thought for sure when the two of you came inside that we were going to get caught."

"You left through the front door?" Misty asked.

"Yes." I nodded.

"Good," she said. "Now, let's go to the store and get the three of you back to the past."

CHAPTER 24

Once we got back to Misty's store, she told her employees they could leave early for the day and turned the sign on the door from "open" to "closed."

"I never close the shop early, but these are special circumstances," she explained. "I've never tried something like this before, so who knows what could happen!"

That didn't sound encouraging.

"Don't look so stressed," she told me. "If the spell works, it will be simple, because the ring should do most of the work. All you need is Chelsea's boost of power, and then you and Drew need to focus on your past lives. Since the ring is strongly connected to your past, the energy created between the three of you and the ring should work its magic and propel you back in time!"

"Oh yeah, totally simple," I said.

The closer we got to doing this, the more I doubted it would work. Now that we were sitting at a table staring at the ring in the center, it was feeling rather silly.

"If you go into it with that attitude, it's only going to be harder," Misty said, her voice soft and understanding. "I know this is a lot to take in, but I imagine everything you've learned in the past few months has been that way as well."

"You're right," I told her. "I didn't believe in past lives until I started remembering my own."

"It goes to show that anything is possible," she said. "You just have to believe."

She sounded like a fairy godmother from a Disney movie, but she did have a point.

"Now, are you ready to start?" she asked.

I wasn't sure, but I nodded anyway. I would never feel totally ready for something like this. It was one of those things you had to jump into and pray for the best.

"Great!" Misty said.

"If this does work, what will it be like when we get there?" I asked, figuring it would be best to understand everything before venturing forward. I wanted to be as prepared as possible. "Like, before we try anything, should we dress in clothes from the time? I wouldn't want to get there and have people freak out because they don't know what jeans are, or why a woman would be wearing something that wasn't a dress."

"Don't worry about that," Misty said. "If it works, the three of you will be propelled into the bodies of your past selves, so you'll be wearing what they were wearing on the day you travel back to."

"Okay." At least that was one less thing I would have to worry about. "So if we're in their bodies, we'll have to trick everyone into believing that we're our past selves. Won't they get suspicious?"

Misty didn't look concerned. "You should have enough memories from your past that this won't be a problem, and you should recall your memories faster once you arrive. If anyone notices something is off, just say you have a headache and aren't feeling like yourself. Plus, if this goes as planned, you shouldn't be there for too long. You're going back to the day of the party when the carriage accident occurred. All you have to do is stop the accident, and then the three of you will gather around the ring again and do the same thing you're about to do now to get back home. You should only be in 1815 for a few hours, max."

When she put it like that, it didn't sound too bad.

"All right," I said, even though I wasn't one hundred percent confident about all this. "I'm ready."

"You each need to put the thumb of your dominant hand on the ring," Misty instructed.

We were all righties, so we put our right thumbs on the ring.

"Why our thumbs?" Chelsea asked.

"The thumb has the strongest pulse of all the fingers," Misty explained. "It's the most powerful for a ritual like this."

I supposed that made sense. My thumb was currently on the part of the ring with the garnets on it, and I could feel a pulse coming from it, like it had a life of its own.

Misty lit four purple candles, and the smell of lavender filled the room. "Once I turn the lights off, I want Drew and Lizzie to think about the day of the party when the accident occurred, and for Chelsea to harness the temporary magic she received from the witch in America. All three of you need to focus on putting your energy into the ring, and accepting the energy from it. Are you ready?"

"Yes," I said with Chelsea and Drew, my voice trembling.

The lights went off, the dim flickers of the candles filling the room. I closed my eyes and focused on the day of the party.

What was I doing that day? I remembered preparing to get ready, but the most important event was Drew giving me the ring when he secretly visited me in my backyard. I was supposed to be dressing for the ball, and his visit made it so I was late to the party, but it was worth it. Because when he gave me the ring and told me he wanted to marry me, it was the happiest moment of my life.

Suddenly my stomach flipped, like it does on roller coasters when you go down the big drop and gravity pulls you so fast that your stomach rises to your throat. I think I screamed, but I couldn't say for sure, because every sound around me disappeared. For a few seconds it was silent, and it was frightening.

Then birds chirping filled my ears, and cold wind blew across my cheeks. Despite the cold, sunlight warmed my skin, and I took a deep breath of crisp winter air. Once my stomach settled, I opened my eyes, and found that I was looking straight into Drew's.

Except this wasn't Drew as he looked in the present. His eyes were the same, but his hair was longer, and his clothes were from two hundred years ago.

This was the Drew from my past.

Meaning the spell had worked, and I was in 1815 England.

CHAPTER 25

"Drew?" I said his name softly, hoping that even though he looked like past-Drew, my Drew was inside there.

"It worked," he said, his dark eyes lighting up in amazement. "I can't believe it worked."

I looked down at my hand, where the garnet ring was displayed on my ring finger. "This was the moment when you asked me to marry you, and I said yes," I said breathlessly.

"That's how I remember it," he said. "Unless you plan on changing your mind?"

"Never!" I said with a laugh.

"Remember, we agreed not to tell anyone we're engaged until the gossip settles about my no longer being engaged to Catherine," Drew reminded me. "We don't want to embarrass her more than necessary, and our engagement would seem quick if I can't court you properly. You're engaged to James right now, too. The only reason your father won't allow you to break the engagement is because he views James as the best possible option for your future. Once everything settles down with Catherine's family, you can let your parents know that we intend to be married, and they can break your engagement with James so I can court you publicly."

"Of course," I agreed. "But we won't have to worry about anything past tonight, because once we stop the carriage accident we'll go back home."

"That's the plan," Drew said.

Then I realized that just as Drew was no longer in his twenty-first century clothes, I was no longer in mine, either. Instead, I was wearing a lilac cotton dress, although I couldn't feel the material on my skin because there were so many layers of clothing between my body and the actual dress. The fabric was stiff, and scratchy. Clearly dryers and dryer sheets had yet to be invented. We were also speaking with British accents, without having to try. It was strange that my voice didn't sound like me.

"Elizabeth!" someone frantically screamed from the front door of the house.

I turned around to see the baffled face of my mother—not my mom from the present, but the woman I remember being my mother in the past. She wore a light-colored day dress, and her hair was pinned back in a formal way that my present day mom never would have worn. She reached where I was standing with Drew and paused to catch her breath. I put my hand behind my back to hide the ring.

"You failed to mention that Mr. Carmichael would be stopping by this afternoon." She turned to Drew and smiled. "Good day, Mr. Carmichael. To what do we owe this visit?"

"Miss Davenport lost an earring at the dinner my family hosted earlier this week, and I wanted to return it to her before Lord Givens' ball this evening," he said, as though he had planned the excuse from the beginning. Perhaps he had, or maybe his past self had and he remembered the plan.

"How kind of you to stop by yourself," she replied. "I was tending to business in the back of the house and Mr. Davenport was in the library, so we couldn't hear you approach. Otherwise we would have greeted you upon your arrival."

"Please don't concern yourself about it, Mrs. Davenport," Drew said. "I'm sure you're busy with preparations for tonight."

"Yes, we must start dressing for the ball soon," my mother said, and I could tell from her anxious tone that she was feeling rushed. "We do have some time, though. Would you care to join us in the parlor for tea?"

"I wouldn't want to trouble you," Drew said with utmost courtesy. "I only wanted to ensure that Miss Davenport had her earring returned before tonight."

"I'm sure she appreciates it very much," my mother said. "Especially since you troubled yourself to deliver it personally. Don't you, dear?"

"Very much," I said. "Thank you, Drew ... I mean, Mr. Carmichael."

My mother looked horrified at my slip-up.

We finished our good-byes, and Drew set off on his horse to return to his estate. Once my mother and I got inside the house, she slammed the door and grabbed me by the arm.

"Calling Mr. Carmichael by his Christian name!" she exclaimed, fanning her face as though what I'd said had shocked her that much. "And the two of you hardly know each other! What has gotten into you? I can only hope he doesn't repeat this mistake to anyone. It could be quite grave ..."

"I forgot myself for a moment," I apologized. "I've been looking forward to the ball tonight so much that it made it difficult to sleep last night, and I'm rather tired. Although," I said, more than willing to change the subject, "Mr. Carmichael did tell me something quite interesting." I was gradually remembering more about my mother from the past, and one major trait I recalled was that if anything was going to distract her, it was some really juicy gossip.

She looked intrigued. "And what is that?"

"Mr. Carmichael has broken his engagement with the Lady Catherine," I said, excitement flooding my veins when my mother's mouth opened in shock. "He says he doesn't love her, and he suspects her motives for marrying him were based purely on his wealth, opposed to his own person."

"Heavens!" my mother exclaimed. "Everyone knows her family needs the money, and his the title. They were supposed to be a perfect match. But more importantly—he chose to call on you personally to return your earring and inform you of this news?"

I wanted to tell her it was because he had proposed to me, but I reminded myself of what Drew had told me when we arrived. No one knew about our secret interludes. If we let them know now, it would be obvious that we had gone behind Catherine's back, and it would look bad for my reputation. Plus, Drew had to approach my father with his intentions so my engagement with James could be broken properly.

But I *could* plant the idea in my mother's head. Because if the plan worked tonight, and we succeeded in stopping my death, Drew and I would get married in the past ... well, in what would now be the future.

And then we could have a future when we returned home.

"I believe it's important for Mr. Carmichael to marry for love," I told my mother. "He doesn't love the Lady Catherine."

"And he cared enough about your thoughts on the matter to deliver the news himself?"

I felt myself blush. "I believe so."

"Now that he is no longer engaged, Mr. Carmichael would be quite the catch—even more so than Mr. Williams," my mother said thoughtfully.

"He would be," I agreed.

"This certainly changes things," she said, and I saw a glint in her eyes that meant she was devising a plan. "Now, we mustn't delay in preparing for the ball. Tell Taylor to get your new dress ready. You need to look your best tonight! And be sure to wear the earring that Mr. Carmichael took time delivering to you today—you wouldn't want to seem ungrateful for his troubles."

"No, I wouldn't," I said before hurrying up to my room to prepare for the night ahead. "I wouldn't at all."

CHAPTER 26

I'd always imagined that preparing for a ball in the Regency Era would be a spectacular experience. It looked so elegant on television and the movies.

Unfortunately, I discovered that as lovely as the clothing and hairstyles were back then, they were severely lacking in modern conveniences that I was accustomed to in the twenty-first century. I missed the minty freshness of Crest toothpaste, and smooth conditioner for my hair. At least my maid, Taylor, wrestled with the tangles and was able to somewhat tame my curls.

Also, the bath was the first I'd taken in years. While it was pleasant, I couldn't imagine a world without showers. This bath was only for the special occasion of the ball, and while I wasn't sure how often people bathed in the Regency Era, it certainly wasn't daily. I wondered if they felt dirty all the time, but I supposed they didn't know the difference.

When I finished getting ready, I was pleased with the outcome. The light-blue dress matched my eyes, and the gloves that traveled up to my elbows made me feel elegant—like I was a real Regency lady. Taylor did my hair in a gorgeous up-do, pinning my curls to my head and leaving a few stray strands to frame my face.

I wore the garnet ring under my glove, and hoped no one would notice it. It would be less suspicious to leave it in my jewelry box while I was out, but I didn't want to let it out of my sight, since it was the way back to the future.

I traveled to the ball in the coach with my parents. Having my parents together in this life was strange, because in my present day life they had been divorced for years. But divorce didn't happen as often in the 1800's. I tried not to think about it too much, though. This wasn't really my life—my real life waited for me in New Hampshire in the twenty-first century. However, the ball we were going to would be the only time I would have such an experience. I was determined to enjoy it as much as I could.

When we pulled up to the Givens' estate, I wondered how they paid for it, since the family was having money problems. That was the main reason why Catherine's mother was insistent that she marry Drew—so his fortune could save their family from financial ruin.

Walking inside the marbled foyer felt like stepping onto the set of a period movie. I wanted to admire the elegant furniture as though in a museum, but it was important that I find Drew and Chelsea. The time travel had worked for Drew and he was in the body of his past self, but I couldn't say the same for Chelsea, as I had yet to speak to Catherine.

It didn't take long to find the two of them talking by the dance floor. Catherine looked beautiful in a bright red dress, and Drew seemed at ease in his formal Regency attire, like he was born to wear it.

Once they spotted me, they waved me over. I hurried through the crowd to their side. Not many people stopped me to say hi, and to those who did, I was able to pretend like I knew who they were. No one suspected a thing.

"We need to find somewhere private to talk," Catherine said the moment I approached. She looked similar to Chelsea in present day, except her face was rounder and her hair done up in curls. I had never seen Chelsea do anything with her hair other than iron it straight.

"I'm assuming it worked?" I needed to verify that this was Chelsea I was speaking to, and not Catherine.

"It did." She nodded. "And I've been through an absolute horror. I'll explain when we're alone."

"It's your house," I told her. "Lead the way."

Everyone was so busy dancing and having fun that they didn't notice the three of us going from the ballroom to the library. We received a couple of strange stares, but I tried not to worry about it. It might not be

Regency custom for two women and a man to leave the ballroom to find somewhere private to speak, but I was only going to be here for a few more hours. My past self would find an excuse for my behavior tonight, such as I wasn't feeling well.

Claiming a headache always explained breaches of etiquette for ladies in the novels I read.

Chelsea closed the door behind us when we arrived in the library. Luckily, no one else was in there. They were all probably too busy having fun in the ballroom.

"I arrived at the worst moment ever!" she exclaimed.

She clearly wanted some prodding, so I asked her to continue.

"This is the day Drew told me he was breaking our engagement, and I got here when Catherine was telling her parents," she said. "I couldn't believe how angry they were at her—as though it were her fault! They were telling me I had to do everything in my power to sway him back to me tonight. They nearly cancelled the party, but ultimately decided it would provide a good opportunity for Drew and I to get back together."

I bit back saying anything. In the past, that was exactly what had happened. Catherine had seduced Drew in this very library, and the moment I saw them together was when I bolted outside and got into my carriage with James at the reins—the carriage that had crashed and caused my death.

"I couldn't believe the amount of pressure they were putting on me," Chelsea said. "They truly believe it's up to me to marry a man rich enough to save our family from financial ruin, as if they weren't the ones who got us in this situation in the first place! I never thought I would say this, but I can't wait to get back home, where all I have to worry about is whether or not I'll get into my top choice college."

I was about to agree with her, but apparently she wasn't done her rant.

"Also, these dresses are pretty, but so uncomfortable. I feel restricted with this much fabric; it's nearly impossible to move without worrying about where each part of my dress is at all times." She put her hands on her hips and huffed, apparently done complaining.

"We'll only be here for a little longer," I told her, trying to calm her down. "All we have to do is make it through the night, and ensure that I arrive home safely. Once tonight is over, we can go home."

"So you're saying we just have to have fun at the party, make sure you get home safe, and then we can go back?" Chelsea seemed relieved at the prospect.

"That's the gist of it," Drew said. "We have to stay until the end of the night to make sure Lizzie goes home with her parents and not James."

"It shouldn't be hard," I added. "There's no way I'm letting James drive me anywhere."

"I suppose it doesn't sound difficult," Chelsea said, although she didn't look thrilled. "Except that I've had a bunch of guys request to dance with me tonight. Most of them are boring, and I would never dance with them at a party at home. But here, a lady isn't allowed to turn down a gentleman when he asks for a spot on her dance card, so I had to say yes. Now I'll have to put up with them all night."

"It's only one night," I said, although I hoped I wouldn't get too many invites to dance that I wanted to turn down, too. Drew was the only person I wanted to dance with, but I remembered enough from my past to know the rules. It was improper for ladies to dance more than two dances with a gentleman, unless they were engaged.

While Drew and I were engaged, it wasn't public, so dancing together all night would be quite the scandal. Doing so would surely complicate matters for my past self once I returned to my own time.

"Instead of counting down the minutes until we're home, we should look at this as a historical experience," I decided. "How many times will we have the opportunity to dance at a real Regency ball? We should appreciate it while we're here."

And appreciate it I did.

* * *

My favorite parts of the night were the two dances I shared with Drew, but the dances with the other gentlemen were not as torturous as Chelsea had made them sound. The men were quite proper; they engaged me in pleasant conversation, and none of them made any inappropriate moves. It was a welcome change from how guys expected girls to be all over them on the dance floor in the twenty-first century.

Once James arrived, the two of us shared three dances, since we were engaged and I didn't want to cause a scene by breaking the engagement in public. He had the same easygoing attitude as Jeremy, so I didn't mind spending time with him. I hoped that after our engagement was broken he would find someone good for him. Maybe someone similar to Keelie.

At midnight, supper was served, featuring cold meats, cheeses, bread, and champagne. There were also sweetmeats and pastries, along with coffee and tea.

When the meal was over, it was finally time to leave. I felt good about the mission. The first time this happened, my past self had left the ball before supper. She would have been dead on the side of the road by this time. Now I was here, barely able to hear the storm raging outside above the music and chatter of the party. The worst of the rain had passed, and there was only a drizzle when I looked out the window.

I didn't want to get optimistic too soon, but it felt like I had changed my fate.

Drew approached me at the end of the night. "I requested that your driver inspect your carriage before you leave," he said, softly enough so only I could hear. "To make sure it will be safe to ride."

"Thank you," I said. It was sweet of him to do that, although we both knew the crash happened because of the storm and James pushing the horses to run faster than they should have in the icy weather. "It seems like we succeeded, doesn't it?"

"It does," he said. "But the night isn't over yet. We'll know for sure once you've made it through to tomorrow. Then our past selves can live their lives, and we can go home to ours."

The knowledge that I would finally be safe and not have to worry about my impending death felt freeing and wonderful.

My family's driver, Mr. Patricks, entered the room, and Drew and I walked over to him.

"Mr. Carmichael." He shifted uneasily and cleared his throat.

"Do you have a report on the carriage?" Drew asked.

"I do." He looked at me in concern and returned his focus to Drew. "Perhaps I should share it with you where there are no ladies present."

"Miss Davenport can hear whatever you have to say," Drew said.

"Very well," Mr. Patricks replied. "Although I'm afraid it's not good news."

Drew's eyes hardened. "Continue."

"It's a good thing you requested I inspect the carriage before our departure tonight," Mr. Patricks said nervously. "As it appears it has been tampered with. If anyone were to have taken it back to the Davenport's home, they wouldn't have made it halfway there before suffering what I fear would have been a rather grave accident."

I digested his words, shocked at what this news implied. "You're positive this was someone else's doing?" I asked. "The coach wasn't simply in need of repair from daily use?"

"I am certain." Mr. Patricks frowned, looking offended that I doubted his expertise. "I take great care in managing the upkeep of the carriage. It was in fine condition before leaving for this evening. The only explanation for its current state is that sometime during the festivities, someone went outside and tampered with it."

I opened my mouth, but found myself unable to speak. Someone had tampered with the carriage? Who would do such a thing? Because if this was done on purpose, it meant ...

My head spun at the only possible explanation, and I reached for the nearest end table to steady myself.

"Would you allow me to speak with Miss Davenport for a moment?" Drew asked Mr. Patricks. "In private?"

Mr. Patricks appeared alarmed by the request, and he looked at me to see how to proceed. It went against social protocol for an unmarried man and woman to be alone with no chaperone, but right now I didn't care about protocol. I needed to talk to Drew.

I nodded to Mr. Patricks that I was fine with Drew's request. He didn't look comfortable with the situation, but it wasn't his job to instruct me on how to behave.

"Certainly." He bowed and made his way to the exit. "I'll find Mr. and Mrs. Davenport and speak with them about the delay."

Drew waited for Mr. Patricks to disappear around the corner before speaking.

"You know what this means, don't you?" he asked in a dark voice.

"Yes." I raised my eyes to meet his, unable to believe this revelation. "The crash that was supposed to have happened tonight wasn't an accident."

Drew nodded. From the haunted look in his eyes, I could tell he was as shocked as I was.

As much as I didn't want to say the words aloud, I had to acknowledge the meaning behind this discovery.

"It was murder."

CHAPTER 27

The news of the incident resulted in my parents speaking with Catherine's parents about how to go about fixing the coach and returning home, which allowed Drew, Chelsea, and me to speak privately in the library. We informed Chelsea about the recent discovery, and she looked just as shocked as we were.

"This means we won't be going home tomorrow morning, doesn't it?" she guessed once we finished telling the story.

"Of course that's what it means." Drew looked at her like she was an awful person for thinking anything else. "We can't leave knowing that someone is trying to murder Lizzie."

"We don't know if Lizzie's the one they were after," Chelsea pointed out. "Her parents also rode with her in the carriage, as did the driver. Couldn't it be one of them that this person wants to get rid of?"

I shivered at the way she said it—get rid of. As if a person was a piece of trash that could be discarded.

"I don't mean to be insensitive." Chelsea must have noticed how what she'd said had upset me. "I'm only trying to look at this from all possible angles."

"It was me they were after." I tried to sound as confident as I felt.

"How do you know?" Chelsea asked, her arms crossed.

"It's just a feeling," I said. "The darkness that I felt after you did your spell hasn't gone away. Whoever tried to kill me tonight failed, and I would say it's highly likely that they're not going to give up easily."

"But who would want to kill you?" Chelsea asked. "It doesn't make sense."

"I hate to ask this," I said, "but you would know if it was Catherine, right? Obviously *you* wouldn't want to kill me, but Catherine isn't entirely the same as you, and she has reason to hate me. Especially after Drew broke the engagement with her earlier today, and with the pressure from her parents to marry him."

Chelsea looked shocked that I could suggest such a thing. "Catherine's angry at you because she suspects your relationship with Drew, but we were close friends in those lives, too. Even if she wished you didn't exist because then you wouldn't have messed things up with her and Drew, she would never take action on those thoughts."

"That's what I was hoping," I said, relieved. "But I had to make sure."

"So it wasn't Catherine," Drew said, pacing in the center of the library. "Who else could hate Lizzie so much that they would want her gone?" He stopped pacing, and looked dead on at Chelsea and me. "We're going to get to the bottom of this. And then, we have to bring an end to it before we can go home."

"Bring an end to it, how?" I didn't like the sound of that.

"I don't know," Drew said. "We'll worry about that once we figure out who's behind this."

I wished I'd read more mystery novels instead of the romances I enjoyed. Maybe then I would be better prepared for what we were about to face. As it was now, I had no idea where to start.

A knock on the door brought me out of my thoughts.

"Come in!" Chelsea chirped, as if we hadn't just been discussing how someone wanted to murder me.

"Am I interrupting something?" Catherine's mom, Lady Givens, asked. She swayed when she walked through the door, and the complicated up-do in her dark hair was missing some pins, leading me to believe that she'd had a lot to drink during the course of the evening.

"Miss Davenport was quite distressed after learning about what happened to her family's coach, so the Lady Catherine and I thought it best for her to take a few minutes to collect herself away from prying eyes," Drew said. "Your guests are having an excellent time tonight, and we didn't think it wise to let them know there is something amiss."

"How thoughtful of both of you." Lady Givens gave Drew a grateful smile, and then turned to me. "Miss Davenport, I'm sorry you had to go through such a scare tonight. Lord Givens and I promise to do everything in our power to figure out who is responsible for this. But if you may, I hope that this inconvenience does not become a source of gossip. I wouldn't want anyone to worry about their safe passage home at my future parties."

"I wouldn't dream of it," I told her, figuring my best move to avoid conflict was to go along with what she was saying. "The news shocked me is all, and I needed a few minutes away from the crowd to absorb what had happened."

"Of course, dear," she said with a warm smile. "If you don't feel well enough to travel, you're welcome to stay here for the night. As a close friend of my daughter's, there is always a room open in our home for you."

"Will my parents be staying here as well?" I asked.

"I offered, but they were also distressed over what transpired tonight, and said they would feel better once they returned safely home," she said. "The repairs on your coach should take a few days, so Lord Givens offered to loan your parents our chaise until your coach is deemed fit to ride again."

I plucked from my past self's memory that a chaise had room for only two passengers. That meant Lady Givens was politely giving me no other option but to spend the night, unless I wanted to walk or ride horseback, which would be a death wish in the cold, rainy weather.

"Thank you, Lady Givens," I said, trying to remain as calm as possible. People in this time period seemed to keep their emotions in check much more than people did in the twenty-first century. "That's very kind of you, and you're right that it's best I don't travel tonight. Hopefully the weather will be pleasant enough tomorrow that I can take one of the horses home."

Lady Givens looked appalled at my suggestion of riding horseback. I loved traveling by horse—it was relaxing and freeing—but it was certainly something that her daughter, the Lady Catherine Givens, would never lower herself to do.

"Very well," she said, although it didn't sound like she meant it. "We'll discuss it further in the morning. In the meantime, I'll send a maid to prepare the guest room. And now, as eventful as this evening has been, I must bid goodnight to my guests. If you'll excuse me." She lifted her skirts, and turned to the door.

"Thank you again, Lady Givens," I said as she hurried out of the room. She left the door open, and I could tell from the looks people were giving us as they walked by that we had secluded ourselves in the library for longer than was socially acceptable.

It hadn't been a day since I'd arrived, and I was already becoming a source of gossip.

"She didn't give you much of an option there, did she?" Drew said once Lady Givens was gone.

"No," I said. "I suppose not. But as much as I would prefer to go home, it's a good thing I'm staying here tonight."

"Why is that?" Drew asked.

"Because once the guests leave, Chelsea and I can brainstorm a list of who we think tampered with the carriage, and why."

"I'll think about it tonight, too," Drew said. "Tomorrow I'll stop by during calling hours. Hopefully the three of us will be able to get time alone, without a chaperone who insists on watching our every move."

"We'll figure something out," I said. "I just want to get answers so we can go home."

Both Chelsea and Drew agreed.

Then Lord Givens' personal valet, Mr. Brookes, knocked on the door to inform Drew that his family had their coach ready and was waiting for him to leave. We all said goodnight, and once the remainder of the guests departed, Chelsea and I headed to her room.

Despite my exhaustion from everything that had happened in the past day, we had important things to discuss, so I couldn't go to bed yet. And I was so wound up from it all that I wasn't sure I could if I tried.

CHAPTER 28

After changing into my nightgown, I met Chelsea back in her room. Her room was much larger than the guest room in which I was staying. She had a four-poster bed, an entire area to get ready with a vanity and wardrobe, a carved marble fireplace, a sitting area, and beautiful red drapes adorning the windows. It was much more extravagant than the bedroom my past self had with her family in their modest home.

But I also knew that the Givens' were in financial crisis, and if Chelsea—well, Catherine—didn't find a wealthy husband, they wouldn't be able to keep up their lavish lifestyle for much longer.

"Finally we can talk freely," I said, hopping onto the bed. For a moment it felt like old times again, when

Chelsea and I would hang out in her room and talk for hours.

It only took a look around the room—and at the long, white nightgown I would never wear at home—to remind myself that everything was different now. My life had gone from average to extraordinary in only a few months, and I still couldn't believe that everything I'd experienced was real. Sometimes I thought that when I woke up in the morning, it would be the first day of junior year all over again, and I'd find out that everything I'd thought had happened since then had only been a dream.

"I was thinking about it when getting ready for bed, and the only people who could be responsible are Drew's parents," Chelsea said with absolute finality.

"And why's that?" I asked, even though they were on my list of suspects, too.

"They know that Drew broke the engagement with Catherine, and I can only assume that they know the reason why is because he wants to marry you instead," Chelsea said. "I overheard people gossiping tonight about how his parents want Drew to marry into nobility. I guess they figured that if they got you out of the picture, he would return to the original plan and follow through with marrying Catherine and thus, into a noble bloodline."

Which was exactly what happened in the past, before we changed everything tonight, I thought, although I wasn't so unkind as to say it aloud. Chelsea was still hurting from Drew's breaking up with her because he loved me, and I didn't want to rub it in.

"That was one of my thoughts, too," I said instead. "Also, and please don't take offense to this, but it's only fair that we add your—I mean Catherine's—parents to the list of suspects."

Chelsea leaned away from me. "I don't think they would do something like that," she said. "Besides, I've thought about it too, and to mess with the carriage they would have had to go out in the rain. Which means their clothes would have been wet, and they were dry all night. So it couldn't be them."

"We didn't see Drew's parents either, but I assume they weren't hanging out at the ball with their clothing soaked," I pointed out. "That certainly would have caused a scene. Also, if it were either your parents or Drew's parents, they could have had a servant do the dirty work for them. I don't think their being dry means anything."

"Maybe." Chelsea shrugged. "But I don't think Catherine's parents would do such a thing, especially since you're one of her close friends. Look at how accommodating they were when they realized how distressed you were tonight!"

"I doubt it's one of them," I lied, and Chelsea visibly relaxed. "But we should consider it as an option until we can eliminate them. They know about the broken engagement, and we know the money is important to them. They have plenty of reasons to want me out of the picture."

"I didn't mention you when I told them about the broken engagement." Chelsea was getting defensive. "I just said that Drew broke the engagement, and I didn't know why."

This admission surprised me. I'd assumed Catherine would gladly throw me under the bus if it meant taking less heat from her parents.

"Why didn't you tell them about me and Drew?" I asked.

"Because being ditched for someone else is embarrassing!" she said. "I suppose they'll eventually find out, but it's not easy to admit."

"I guess that makes sense," I said, feeling guilty again for causing her such heartbreak. But at least Chelsea and I were on speaking terms now, which was better than where we were a few weeks ago. "Do you have any other ideas of who it could be?"

"Not that I could come up with," Chelsea said. "Unless James went nuts and decided that if he couldn't have you, then no one else could, either."

I looked at her in shock, unsure if she was serious. "That's gruesome!" I finally said. "He would have to be completely mental to do that."

"I know." Chelsea laughed. "I doubt he's the type to think like that. I just wanted to see the expression on your face when I said it. And trust me, it was priceless."

I tossed a pillow at her head, and she blocked it so it fell off the bed. At least despite everything we were going through, I could still joke around with my best friend.

"So that's it, then," I said. "Four main suspects."

"Yep," Chelsea said. "That's all I could come up with."

"Where do we go from here?" I asked. "We can't file a police report and properly interrogate them. And what if whoever it is tries again?" I shivered at the possibility. The scary truth was that someone wanted me dead, and they had succeeded before the three of us came back to the past and changed how last night ended. Whoever it was had to be desperate to resort to murder, and I doubted they would give up easily.

"You'll have to be on the lookout," Chelsea said. "Be extra cautious before doing anything, and stay with either me or Drew at all times. You're an easier target when you're alone. I promise we're going to figure out who's responsible, and then we can go home."

"That sounds nice," I said, unable to stifle a yawn. This past day had been exhausting, and I had no idea how long it had been since I last slept. Plus, I was still jet lagged from the flight from America to England. "Do you mind if I stay in your room tonight?" I asked, since Catherine's king-sized bed was big enough for both of us. She had also just said that I had to stay with her or Drew at all times, and walking through the halls by myself and sleeping in the guest room alone wasn't the best way to protect myself from whoever wanted me dead.

I doubted anyone would kill me while I was sleeping, but I couldn't be too careful.

"I was actually going to *insist* that you stay in here tonight," Chelsea said. In that moment everything felt like it did in the old days, when we had sleepovers all the time.

We might never be able to go back to that age, but I believed that with Chelsea and Drew's help, we could make it so I would be able to live to see the new year, and many more to come.

CHAPTER 29

As promised, Drew stopped by during afternoon calling hours the next day, presumably to see how I was doing after the scare last night. I wanted to tell him the truth—that I hated watching out with every move I made because I was terrified that whoever wanted me dead would succeed, and that I wanted to go back home to normal life.

Unfortunately, I couldn't speak freely, since social customs dictated that Lady Givens be in the room during calling hours as well. Not only that, but I had to repeat the lie that Lord Givens had told us at breakfast this morning, that further investigation proved the carriage hadn't been tampered with, and the problem was due to the bad weather mixed with the carriage being old and in need of updating.

I didn't believe him for a second. Yes, the carriage was old, but our coachman had been working for our family for years. I knew from exploring what I could of my past self's memories that he wouldn't raise alarm unless he was certain he was correct.

I also wondered about Lord Givens' motivation behind the lie. My first conclusion was that it looked bad to have an attempted murder occur during an event hosted at his house, and he wanted to stop the gossip. But the other, more sinister possibility haunted my thoughts: What if he was behind the attempt and was trying to cover his trail?

It made me antsier to speak with Drew and Chelsea in private. However, Lady Givens seemed so thrilled that Drew had stopped by that I doubted she would be leaving the room any time soon.

Not thirty minutes had passed before Mr. Brookes came into the sitting room and announced that my parents, Mr. and Mrs. Davenport, had stopped by. They seemed relieved to see me. Lady Givens broke the "news" to them about the problem with the carriage being an accident, and as much as I hated the lie, it put my parents at ease. I couldn't imagine what had been going through their minds last night. They had no idea about the relationship between Drew and me, so they must have been confused about why someone would want anybody from our family dead.

Lady Givens switched the topic as soon as she could, asking my parents how they enjoyed the ball. This led to a lengthy discussion of who was wearing what, who said what to whom, and who danced with each other and how many times. It seemed like my mother could gossip with Lady Givens for hours on end.

All I wanted was to speak to Drew and Chelsea alone, but that was looking more and more impossible.

This was made more impossible when James and his parents stopped by. Presumably, they were there to thank Lord and Lady Givens for throwing such a wonderful party, although I suspected they were looking for a way to get James under my skin. I wasn't spending as much time with James since I'd met Drew, and I could tell he was worried that my feelings for him were waning. Which, of course, they were.

I wanted to break the engagement as soon as possible.

But making such a strong, public announcement would only make whoever wanted to kill me more determined to finish the deed. Breaking the engagement would have to wait until the person coming after me was stopped.

The awkward conversation between the group lasted for another hour, although it felt longer. There was also no opportunity for Drew, Chelsea, and me to converse privately. I was bursting with the anticipation of wanting to tell Drew what Chelsea and I had discussed last night, and to hear his opinions, but I had to keep my emotions in check.

I would be able to talk with him eventually. For now, I had to be patient.

"Would you all like to stay for dinner?" Lady Givens asked when the conversation lulled.

"That would be lovely," my mother said. "Thank you."

Mrs. Williams accepted the invitation as well, and Lady Givens left the room to inform the kitchen staff to prepare food for the added guests. I imagined this might cause a frenzy in the kitchens, but no one seemed concerned.

This also meant I would have to sit through a long, drawn out dinner before speaking privately with Drew and Chelsea. It wasn't what I wanted to do, but with the social rules inherent with the early nineteenth century, I had no other option.

At dinner I ended up squished between James and Mr. Williams. I say squished because Mr. Williams was quite a large man—so large that I was surprised his bottom fit on the chair. James didn't seem to have inherited this unfortunate gene, but who knows what could happen in the future.

Lord and Lady Givens arranged it so Chelsea sat next to Drew, and that I was as far away from the two of them as possible. None of this would have seemed odd to anyone—since I was engaged to James—but it angered me. I didn't like being told where to sit. It wasn't my home, though, so I wasn't going to say anything. Plus, in the scheme of things it wouldn't be a big deal.

When the red wine came out, Mrs. Williams raised her glass to make a toast. "To a wonderful party held by Lord and Lady Givens last night, and to the hope of many more fabulous nights to come!" she said.

Everyone raised their glasses and took a sip. I did the same—but only to be polite. I wasn't a big drinker at home. The one time my mom allowed me to have red wine at a nice restaurant, I became fatigued and ended up with a headache for the rest of the night.

I stuck with water instead, hoping no one would notice. I assumed my past self had no trouble drinking wine at meals, since it wasn't illegal for teenagers to drink alcohol in the nineteenth century and she would have grown accustomed to it, but I didn't want to risk it.

"Are you not drinking your wine?" Mr. Williams asked mid-way through the main course. So much for no one noticing.

"I have a slight headache, so I'm only going to be drinking water tonight," I explained.

"Well, we mustn't let a fine glass of wine go to waste!" Mr. Williams said. His ears were bright pink—he'd had a lot to drink, and I suspected he was feeling the effects of the alcohol. "Would you mind if I had yours?"

I told him it was fine. Without delay, he reached for my glass and downed half of its contents in one gulp.

"Oh, honey," Mrs. Williams said quietly, sounding exasperated. "I'm sure the staff wouldn't mind refreshing your wine. There's no need to make a spectacle of yourself by drinking from Miss Davenport's glass."

"Miss Davenport doesn't mind," Mr. Williams said, taking another gulp of the wine. "Right, dear?"

"Right." I nodded, although I agreed with Mrs. Williams that Mr. Williams' drunkenness was causing him to "make a spectacle" of himself. I didn't say it out loud, though.

Lady Givens ordered Mr. Brookes to bring more wine to the table, but not before Mr. Williams had finished my entire glass. When Mr. Brookes asked me if I would like more wine, I said I was fine with water. He didn't look pleased, but that wasn't my problem.

"Do you have any news on the date of Mr. James' and Miss Davenport's upcoming nuptials?" Lady Givens asked Mrs. Williams.

This question led to a long (and for me, unwelcome) discussion of possible dates and locations for the wedding. The mothers were excited to discuss every detail, and their husbands seemed more than happy to take the time to properly enjoy their meat.

Only Drew, Chelsea, and I knew that this wedding would never happen.

"You've been quiet this evening, my dear," Mrs. Williams observed, looking at me in concern. "Is everything all right?"

"Everything is fine," I said. "I just have a slight headache, is all."

Unlike earlier, when I had used the same excuse for my reason of not drinking wine, now it was the truth. I wondered if the headache could be from the wine, although I doubted it, since I'd only had a sip. I was probably just stressed from everything that had happened recently.

"I hope you're not coming down with anything," she said. "You had quite a scare last night. I'm sure we're all glad that's been cleared up."

"Yes, very much so," I said, although the mention of the almost-accident put me on edge once more. "So much has happened in the past day. I'm sure I'll feel better in the morning."

"I do hope so, dear," she said before taking another sip of her wine.

Luckily, that ended the conversation about the wedding. But unluckily, it seemed like it was going to be impossible to get time alone with Chelsea and Drew. This meal felt like it was lasting forever. I was glad when the main course ended and dessert was served, and while I was full from the meal, I ate some fruit to be polite.

"Now that the weather is better, we can attach the side seat to the chaise so Elizabeth can come home tonight," my mother said once we finished dessert. Then she turned to Lady Givens. "Thank you again for lending it to us. I hope it won't be long until our coach is repaired."

"It was no trouble," Lady Givens assured her. "Your coach should be ready within a few days. I am terribly sorry for the inconvenience."

"Oh, but it's not your fault," my mother said. "I'm just glad my coachman inspected the carriage before taking us home. Imagine what could have happened if we hadn't known it needed a repair!"

"Yes," Lady Givens said. "It would have been quite grave, indeed."

When dinner ended, Lady Givens led the women to the drawing room, while the men stayed behind in the dining room to continue drinking and talking. The mothers walked ahead, leaving Chelsea and I to follow.

"When are we going to get time to talk to Drew?" Chelsea whined, quietly enough so only I could hear. "I feel like I'm being baby-sat all the time here."

"I'm getting annoyed, too," I said. "All this protocol is making it impossible for us to do what we have to."

"I just want to fix this mess and go home," she said.

"We had no way of knowing everyone would stop by tonight," I said. "It made everything a million times more difficult. It might be best to wait for tomorrow. We can meet up in the yard behind my house and talk there."

"I guess we don't have another choice," Chelsea said in defeat. "We'll have to get word to Drew."

Which was exactly what we did when everyone was saying goodnight.

I hoped we would come to a solid plan tomorrow, because as fascinating as this experience was, I was more than ready to go home.

CHAPTER 30

As planned, Drew and Chelsea met up with me in the yard behind my house the following afternoon. Chelsea and I briefed Drew on our list of possible suspects, and asked for his opinion.

"I was thinking along those same lines," he said. "And my mom told me something interesting before I left today."

"What?" I asked, anxious for him to continue.

"She ran into Mrs. Williams this morning while shopping in town, and Mrs. Williams said that Mr. Williams had been terribly ill all night. He blamed it on the food at dinner, but no one else got sick."

"Sounds like he got a bug," I said. "Or maybe ..."

"Maybe what?" Chelsea asked.

"I only took a small sip of my wine, but I wasn't feeling one hundred percent last night," I said. "I thought it was nerves because of the pressure of what we have to do here. But Mr. Williams drank my entire glass when I said I wasn't feeling up to drinking."

"So you think someone put something in your wine?" Chelsea's eyes widened. "That's absurd!"

"Is it?" I asked. "I'm not an expert on poisons, but I would guess that the amount needed to kill me wouldn't be lethal to Mr. Williams, who must be triple my size. It would only make him ill."

"Possibly," Chelsea said. "But I don't think we have enough evidence to assume anything."

"It is something to think about, though," I said.

"And you're not going to like the second part of what she said," Drew continued.

I looked at him in dread. "There's more?"

"My mom convinced Mrs. Williams that she should host an engagement party for you and James on Saturday night."

"But that's not even a week away!" I said, horrified. "I was hoping the engagement would be broken by then— not that we would be celebrating."

"I knew you wouldn't like it," Drew said.

"We'll have to make sure this party doesn't happen," I concluded. "It's only going to make things harder and more embarrassing for everyone involved when the truth comes out."

"Or we could use the party as a way to get the answers we need," Chelsea suggested.

"What do you mean?" I asked.

"Everyone involved will be there," she said. "We'll just have to corner the suspects, and get one of them to admit to what they're trying to do."

"I doubt it will be that easy," I said.

"But we have to try," she insisted. "Unless either of you has a better idea?"

I didn't, and I looked at Drew to see his reaction.

"I have an idea," he said. "But it's going to cause quite the commotion."

I leaned forward, intrigued. "And what is this idea?"

He shared his plan with Chelsea and me. At first I was shocked, but then I realized it was so crazy it might work.

"I can't believe I'm agreeing to this, but if we want to do this right, it needs to be dramatic," I said. "Saturday night we're getting to the bottom of this. And then we're going home."

CHAPTER 31

The days leading up to the celebration were rather dull. The family would awaken around eight, and we would read books and write letters until breakfast at ten. I learned that the "morning hours" were defined differently from what I was accustomed to in modern times. In the Regency Era, "morning" was the time until dinner, which was served around five.

Dinner was the longest meal of the day, consisting of two to three courses. It could last for two to three hours. We would always dress for the meal, even though we were only dining with family.

I spent most of my free time reading, sketching, doing needlework, and practicing the pianoforte. The most exciting thing that happened was going into town with my mother to shop for ribbons to update my dresses.

Country living was peaceful, but I felt disconnected from the world. I missed the convenience of my computer and cell phone. It was also hard to relax knowing that on Saturday night I would have to work with Drew and Chelsea to figure out who was after me once and for all.

The repairs on the family coach were finished on Friday, so my parents returned the chaise to the Givens' and got the coach back in our possession. The Givens' invited us to dinner, and while my parents went, I refused the invitation, claiming I wasn't feeling well and wanted to make sure I was in peak condition for the ball tomorrow night. In truth, I was so stressed over what I had to do at the ball that I doubted I would be agreeable company.

Finally, Saturday arrived. It took longer than usual for my maid to get me ready, since I was the guest of honor. I wore my nicest white dress, and Taylor did my hair in a braided, elaborate up-do, adding a headpiece of interspersed pearls.

I wished I could recreate the look once I got home, but I doubted I could do it justice.

"You're going to have a marvelous time tonight," Taylor said once she finished getting me ready. "I can't wait to hear all about it."

My hands shook, and I wished she was right—that tonight would be the kind of wonderful that happened in fairy tales. My life recently *had* felt like a fairy tale, but at the same time, it also felt like the opposite. How was I supposed to stop someone who wanted me out of the picture? How did I get in so over my head?

"Are you all right, Miss Elizabeth?" Taylor asked.

"I'm fine," I said, regaining my composure. "I suppose the excitement is getting to me."

I wanted to confide in her about my secret engagement to Drew and breaking the engagement with James, but I knew better than that. The maids gossiped, especially Taylor, even though she was a sweetheart. Sharing a big secret with her would ensure that everyone in Hampshire County knew the news within a week.

"You're going to be the most beautiful lady there," she said. "No one will be able to take their eyes off you all night."

"Thank you," I said, although there was only one person there who I hoped to impress, and his name was Andrew Carmichael.

* * *

My parents complimented me on my choice of dress for the evening (although Taylor was the one who decided it was perfect for the event), and we boarded the coach. It was eerie being inside of there, knowing that if we hadn't succeeded in going back in time, the coach would be shattered beyond repair, and instead of going to a party tonight, everyone would have been attending my funeral.

I tried to stay positive, though. Being here was proof that I had the power to control my destiny. I could make it so my past self lived out the life she deserved, and then go back home and live the life I deserved, too.

Maybe I would get my fairy tale ending, after all.

CHAPTER 32

The ball was a splendid affair. The Williams' home wasn't as extravagant as the Givens', but they had a large ballroom, and they went all out with getting an orchestra and hiring extra staff to make sure the attendees had a drink in their hand whenever they weren't on the dance floor.

As expected, James and I began the starting dance. It was a lively country dance, as most of them were, and we had fun, in a friends way. That was how my relationship with James felt—like we were friends, and nothing more.

Just as Jeremy was able to get over our relationship quickly, I had a feeling that James would be the same way once I broke the engagement. At least I hoped so, knowing what was about to happen tonight.

The dance ended, and I thanked James, telling him I would be right back. Really, I searched the crowd for Drew and Chelsea. My heart was beating so fast that if I didn't know any better, I would think everyone in the room could hear it. They would all know I was about to do something crazy that went against the social rules of Regency Era, England.

But while I had a past life here, I was from the twenty-first century. If my past self needed some modernity to make her life the way it should be, then that was exactly what was going to happen.

I was going to get that happily ever after—in both my past life *and* my present.

I found Drew and Chelsea standing by the interior wall of the ballroom, where they had promised they would be waiting.

"Are you ready?" Drew asked, holding his arm out for me to take.

I put my arm through his, trying to stop from shaking. "As I'll ever be."

"Relax." He leaned closer so his lips touched my ear. "I love you, always and forever. This will work, and you'll be safe once and for all. Then we'll go back home, and our lives can return to normal."

"Normal." I laughed. "I feel like I don't know what that is anymore."

"It'll be the two of us, together," he said. "Like it was meant to be."

"I love you," I said, soft enough so only he could hear. "Always and forever." I surveyed the crowd once more, and my confidence grew. It was now or never. "Okay. I'm ready."

CHAPTER 33

The first step of the plan was easily completed—Drew and I danced four dances together, in a row. It was wonderful dancing with him, but by the end of the third dance, when we started the fourth, the whispers began.

People were wondering what we were doing, spending the amount of time together that one should only spend with the person they are engaged to marry. I caught looks of disapproval from the corner of my eye, but I didn't care. Drew was the one I loved and wanted to be with. Who I *would* be with.

This wasn't the most proper way to announce it, but it was certainly getting the attention we desired.

By the end of the fourth dance, my mother approached us. She looked regal and stoic, but a storm brewed in her eyes. Clearly she was not about to allow Drew and I to spend a fifth dance together.

I hoped that four dances gave Chelsea enough time to complete her part of the plan.

"What are the two of you doing?" my mother sternly asked Drew and me.

By this point, nearly everyone who had been on the dance floor was staring at us, and the dancing had come to a halt.

"I would like to make an announcement," Drew said, since he had the attention of nearly everyone attending the party. Those who were not watching before turned to listen. "As many of you are aware, I recently broke my engagement with the Lady Catherine Givens." The crowd gave a collective gasp, and he continued, "I did not break the engagement because of anything done wrong on her behalf—Lady Catherine is a lovely person—but I could not marry her because I do not love her. I could not marry her because I am in love with Miss Elizabeth Davenport."

This declaration was met with dropped jaws and complete silence. Now he really had the crowd's attention.

I met their eyes with confidence, prepared for what Drew was going to say next, but he was interrupted before he had a chance.

"What is the meaning of this?" Mrs. Williams' asked, stomping onto the dance floor. She held her dress in her hands, her expression twisted into horror. "You know very well that Miss Davenport is promised to my son,

Mr. James Williams. This party is to honor their engagement, for Heavens sake!"

James rushed to my side, although the defeated look in his eyes showed me that he knew this battle was lost. But that didn't stop him from trying.

"Mr. Carmichael, you need to leave this party at once," James commanded.

"But they have already danced four dances together!" Mrs. Williams cried. "This is disastrous." Then she turned to me. "Miss Davenport, you do intend to marry my son, correct?"

I wished things could be different and I could say what she wanted to hear to put her at ease, but I had my future happiness to consider.

"I'm sorry, but I cannot," I said, turning to James. "I hope you understand that I value your friendship greatly, but I do not love you. I've loved Mr. Carmichael since the night I met him, and for that reason, I fear I cannot marry you." I stepped away from James, and closer to Drew. "Please believe me when I tell you that I trust this will make us both happier in the end," I told James. Hopefully he would forgive me in time. I wouldn't blame him if he didn't—I hated that it had to come to this, and especially that we had to do this so publicly.

It had to be done, though. We didn't have endless time on our hands, and a dramatic revealing of my relationship with Drew seemed the best bet to evoke strong emotions from whoever wanted me dead. And it seemed like we had succeeded. Everyone was speechless—clearly this wasn't the sort of entertainment they saw every day.

James didn't look too upset, however, and Mrs. Williams ushered him away.

My father pushed to the front of the crowd before this could continue. I hadn't searched for him until now, because I was terrified of his reaction. I feared he would be livid. But to my surprise, I didn't find anger on his aging features. Instead, he seemed amused by the situation.

"Mr. Carmichael," my father said with a hint of a smile. "Before this proceeds any further, I believe there's something you would like to ask me?"

"Of course." Drew stood straighter and cleared his throat. Then he looked my father in the eyes and said, "I've loved your daughter since the moment I saw her, and the love I feel for her has only grown since. There's no one else I could foresee spending the rest of my life with, and for that reason, I would like to respectfully ask for your consent in my requesting her hand in marriage."

"Very well." My father nodded, and turned to me. "Do you love Mr. Carmichael?"

"Yes." I didn't have to think about my answer. "I do. Very much so."

"Well, I do wish this had been done more discreetly," my father began. "Although I must say, I haven't had such an entertaining evening in years. Since it seems obvious that the two of you love each other, I suppose I don't have much of a choice but to grant my permission."

"You're not mad?" I couldn't believe my luck. Even though this man was Elizabeth Davenport of the past's father and I didn't know him as well as my own, I was glad he wasn't furious at the turn of events of the evening. In fact, he seemed pleased that marrying Drew would make me happy.

"I do wish you had explained your feelings sooner, and more privately," he said. "Perhaps this could have been resolved in a cleaner manner. But I do believe Mr. Carmichael loves you, and if you promise that this is truly what you want, then I am most definitely happy for you."

"As I am, as well," my mother chimed in.

Then Drew did something that was unheard of for this time period—he kissed me in public, for everyone to see. The kiss was short, but it took my breath away just the same.

"We've really changed the past, haven't we?" I asked once the kiss ended.

"We have," Drew said. "But it's not over yet."

"No," I said, not wanting to put a damper on the moment, but knowing I had to. I lowered my voice before continuing, "Whoever's after me is probably a hundred times angrier after witnessing what just happened."

This was where things were going to get tricky. The entire party had been arranged to celebrate my and James' engagement, and we had to ensure the party continued now that the engagement was cancelled and everyone knew I was engaged to Drew.

It came down to if Chelsea had succeeded with her part of the plan.

"Let's find Mrs. Williams," Drew said.

* * *

Mrs. Williams wasn't a scary woman by any means, but I was afraid to confront her. After all, I had just humiliated her son in public by announcing that I was in love with someone else during our engagement. She would have every right to hate me and cancel the party on the spot.

Drew must have noticed I was nervous, because he took my hand and squeezed it. "It's going to be okay," he said. "Tomorrow we'll be home, and this will all be in the past."

"I hope so," I said.

It wasn't hard to find Mrs. Williams. She stood near the entrance to the ballroom, frantically fanning herself while talking with the circle of supporters surrounding her. She looked stressed, but I suspected she thrived on this kind of drama.

Drew and I approached, and everyone talking with her quieted.

"Would it be all right for Miss Davenport and I to speak with Mrs. Williams?" Drew asked.

The question was met with nods and mutterings of "of course," before everyone scurried in different directions. The three of us stepped into the hall for privacy.

"Mrs. Williams," I said, feeling a rush of guilt just from looking at her. I may not know her personally, but she was close to my past self. "I'm sorry for the turn of events tonight. I wish things could have been different. I understand if you want us to leave, or if you want to end the party entirely."

"No, no, my dear," she said, shushing me and shaking her head. "I mean, yes, at first that was what I thought I would have to do. But then I saw James dancing with Miss Kate Duncan, and they were having such a splendid time together that I wouldn't dream of calling off the party!"

I smiled, because if what she was saying was true, then Chelsea had succeeded. I also wasn't surprised that Mrs. Williams was pleased—Kate Duncan came from a wealthier, more respected family than my past self did, which was important to people in this time-period.

Actually, I supposed it was important to people in modern times as well, although not nearly as intensely so.

"Please believe me when I say I'm sincerely happy for him," I said. "I think Miss Duncan will be a wonderful match for him."

"Me too, me too," Mrs. Williams said. "And congratulations to the both of you!" She smiled at me, and then turned to Drew. "Please don't repeat this, but once you get past titles, I can happily vouch for Miss Davenport's character over Lady Catherine's any day."

"I agree with you, and I'll be certain to not say a word," Drew said, his eyes twinkling in amusement.

"If you'll excuse me, I have to check on my guests, but I hope the two of you have a lovely time tonight," Mrs. Williams said. Then she leaned forward and lowered her voice. "I'm looking forward to the wedding. I'm sure it will be more lavish than anything this town has seen in years!"

With that, she left and met up with the group she had been gossiping with before Drew and I approached her.

Chelsea must have been watching us talking, because it wasn't long until she joined us in the hall.

"You did it?" I asked.

"Yep," she said proudly. "It wasn't hard. I was able to recreate the potion Alistair showed me how to make that we gave to our parents to convince them to let us come to England—the one that opens people's minds. Once I put some in James' drink, he was completely open to the idea that Kate was a better match for him than you. He had apparently been interested in her for the past few weeks, just as Jeremy was interested in Keelie, but didn't say anything until you broke up with him. I found him in the middle of the first dance you and Drew shared, and by the time everything was revealed, he seemed *happy* that the engagement was off so he could pursue Kate!"

"I'm glad that worked out," I said, although my stomach fluttered at the knowledge of what I had to do next. I could be putting my life on the line—again.

I wasn't sure I was ready for this.

"Everything will be fine," Drew said. "Remember that I'll be right behind you, so if anything dangerous happens I can stop it."

"I trust you," I said. "Let's do this."

I might have sounded prepared, but I didn't feel that way at all.

CHAPTER 34

It took a while for us to find the perfect time to enact the plan, when Catherine's parents and Drew's parents were both in hearing distance from the three of us. The four of them didn't look pleased with the events of the night, but they were doing their best to pretend like they were happy. They weren't doing a great job, but the other guests were too busy dancing and enjoying the refreshments to notice.

Drew let me know that now was the time.

"I'm getting a bit of a headache," I said, loudly enough that everyone within a ten foot radius could hear. Of course, this radius included Drew's and Catherine's parents. "I'm going to step outside in the garden for a few minutes to get some air."

"Do you want me to go with you?" Drew asked.

"Thank you for offering, but no," I said, plastering a smile on my face. "Stay inside and enjoy yourself. This night has been so eventful—a few minutes by myself to process it all will be good."

"As you wish," Drew said. "I'll be in here waiting for you."

"I'll see you soon."

As I headed outside, I walked past Drew's parents and Catherine's parents, where they stood talking with each other and a few other guests.

"Are you all right, dear?" Mrs. Carmichael asked me. She sounded genuinely concerned.

"I'm fine." I smiled. "I just have a slight headache, so I'm going to step outside for a few minutes to get some air."

She looked like she wanted to say more, but she didn't, instead giving me her wishes for me to feel better.

I thanked her and walked past the groups of guests chatting and drinking. Many heads turned in my direction as I walked by. I supposed the drama earlier that evening was making me somewhat of a celebrity for the night.

The harsh cold of the winter night struck my face when I stepped outside. Luckily, the layers of my dress kept me from completely freezing. I was unsurprised that the inclement weather was keeping the other guests from dallying in the gardens. Anyone with sense would stay inside.

This garden was smaller than the one at Drew's grandparents house, and unlike when we walked through that garden, this one was not covered in snow. The only signs of life were the interspersed evergreens. I saw spots where flowers would bloom in the warmer seasons, but now they were bare.

A stone fountain gurgled in the center of the garden, and I sat on the bench across from it, preparing for whatever was going to happen next. The bench was far enough from the house that no one could see me through the door or window, which made it the perfect place for me to wait.

Biding my time, I looked up at the stars, the twinkling dots millions of light years away connecting me from this time-period to mine. The Big Dipper and Orion's Belt looked the same as they did in the twenty-first century. I loved looking at the stars—they put in perspective how small I was compared to the Universe. Each of those hundreds of billions of stars was its own sun. It could have its own solar system of planets orbiting around it, and some of those planets could even contain life.

The vastness of possibilities in space reminded me that while my life felt important, it was tiny in the scheme of things. Human civilization was only a blink on the radar of time.

Did anyone else have these moments of amazement over the existence of humanity, when they are in awe of how they are here, and alive, even if it's only for a short while?

I wished on my favorite star, the middle one of Orion's Belt, that everything would work out tonight.

"Miss Davenport," a female voice pulled me from my thoughts. "I do hope you're feeling all right?"

I looked up and saw Catherine's mother, Lady Givens, holding her skirts as she walked toward me. Her question was one of concern, but it didn't sound like she cared.

"Lady Givens," I greeted her. "I'm fine, thank you for asking. I only needed a few minutes by myself to take in all that has happened this evening."

"It has been quite ... dramatic," she said with distaste. "Do you mind if I sit with you?"

"Not at all." I scooted to the edge of the bench to give her room. What was she up to? I felt like it wasn't something good, but her presence put me in no danger. She couldn't do anything other than attack me with words. I refused to allow her to get to me.

"Did you come out here because you're having second thoughts about your engagement to Mr. Carmichael?" she asked. She looked flushed—I couldn't tell if it was because of anger or the icy breeze—and her eyes flickered with hate when she said the word engagement. "I wouldn't blame you if you are."

"Why would you say that?" I asked.

"He's clearly torn between you and Catherine," she said. "It's obvious that given time he'll come to terms with his mistake, break his engagement with you, and everything will continue as it was meant to be."

"By 'meant to be,' you mean him being with Catherine?" Anger rose in my chest at that she dared say such a thing.

"Why, of course." She smiled, although it was filled with malice.

"That's not going to happen," I said, my tone sharp. "Drew loves me, and the two of us *will* be married."

"Surely you see why it's more practical for him to marry Catherine," Lady Givens said.

"But he doesn't love Catherine," I said, more forcefully now. "He loves me. And I love him. I'm sorry for Catherine, truly, but she will eventually meet the right person for her."

"It's a pity it has to be this way," Lady Givens said with a shake of her head.

"What do you mean?"

"Mr. Brookes?" Lady Givens called the name of Lord Givens' personal valet. "It's time."

Before I knew what was happening, Mr. Brookes emerged from the shadows and secured one arm around my shoulders, pinning me to the bench. He wrapped his other hand around my mouth to stop me from screaming. I squirmed to try and escape, but he was too strong for me to fight.

Then Lady Givens pulled a small knife from her glove, the silver glinting in the moonlight. Her eyes had a wild rage to them, like an animal about to pounce.

I tried turning my head to get out of Mr. Brookes' grip, but it was no use. I was trapped. I couldn't even scream for help.

I would have been more terrified if I didn't know that Drew had followed me outside to help in an emergency. What was he waiting for? I shouldn't worry, though. He would come to my rescue at any second.

Lady Givens toyed with the knife and cocked her head to the side, watching me with a twisted smile. "I really did like you, Elizabeth," she said. "Until you stole my daughter's one chance at happiness—her chance to make sure her family was protected for the rest of our lives. If Catherine doesn't marry Mr. Carmichael, it will be the end of everything. Our lives will be over. We'll have to sell the estate, the coaches ... we'll be destitute. This was our final chance. And then you had to ruin it." She was looking at me with absolute hatred. "It will be so sad when you're found in the gardens, having slit your wrists because you couldn't handle the guilt of betraying your ex-fiancé and closest friend. Then, with you out of the picture, Mr. Carmichael will surely return to his original promise to marry Catherine."

I wanted to say that no one would believe her and that her plan was crazy, but it came out as a muffled noise against Mr. Brookes' fleshy palm.

Lady Givens held the knife closer to my wrists, tracing a delicate line on top of my gloves. I wasn't sure if she would go through with it, but you never knew what people would do when they felt like their entire existence was threatened.

I looked around, starting to panic. Where was Drew? He should be here by now. I kicked my feet to try to break free, but it was no use. I was stuck. If Drew didn't get here soon, Lady Givens might go through with this insane plan, and I would be right back to where things had ended originally—lifeless, outside in the cold, surrounded by pools of my own blood.

Finally, just when I thought something had happened and Drew hadn't followed me, he stepped through the hedges and into the opening.

"Put the knife down, and let her go," he commanded. His voice was steady, although his eyes raged with anger.

"Oh, Mr. Carmichael!" Lady Givens laughed—an evil cackling sound that reminded me of a witch from a fairy tale. "How nice of you to join us."

"Did you not hear me the first time?" He took a step closer. "Put the knife down and let Elizabeth go."

"You misunderstand." Lady Givens' voice was sickly sweet. "This isn't what it looks like."

She didn't have time to explain, because I used that moment to slam my head back into Mr. Brookes' face.

His grip on me faltered, and I bolted from where I'd been pinned to the bench to stand next to Drew. He put his arm protectively around me, pulling me close. My head hurt from the impact on Mr. Brookes' jaw, but I would worry about that later.

"It was exactly what it looked like," I said now that I was safely out of Mr. Brookes' hold.

"You're lying," Lady Givens accused through clenched teeth. "Besides, who's going to believe your word over mine? I'm from one of the oldest, most well-respected families in this town, and you're from absolutely nothing."

"I heard the entire thing," Drew said. "And we know this wasn't the first time you've tried to hurt Miss Davenport. You made sure her carriage would be tampered with, and if I had to bet on it, I would say you put something in her wine that night we dined at your home. It was only by mistake that Mr. Williams drank it instead."

Lady Givens paled, and said nothing.

"But clearly you couldn't do this on your own," I said, turning my attention to Mr. Brookes. "The big question is—what did *you* have to gain from this?"

"If Lord and Lady Givens have no money, I'm out of a job." He rubbed his jaw, which must hurt after I'd whammed it with the back of my head. "My Lady is quite observant, and she wasn't blind to Mr. Carmichael's affections for you. I was promised a substantial raise if I helped get you out of the picture so Mr. Carmichael would continue with the plan to marry Lady Catherine. I just had no idea the task would prove so difficult."

Lady Givens was still as pale as ever, looking like she was about to throw up. I assumed she was in shock.

Then she stood from the bench, raised the knife, and launched herself toward me, her eyes ablaze with hatred. But she wasn't threatening or fast in her party dress, and I easily stepped out of her reach. Drew used the opportunity to grab her arm and pull the knife from her hands.

She looked back and forth between us in malice.

"What do you plan on doing now?" she asked Drew. "Ruin me more than you already have?"

"I didn't fall in love with Elizabeth to spite Catherine and the rest of your family," he said. "I'm sorry you're having financial trouble, but I'm not to blame for it, and Elizabeth certainly isn't responsible."

Lady Givens huffed, clearly not agreeing with that statement.

Drew ignored her, and continued, "Here's what's going to happen now. You will stop going after Elizabeth, and you will let us live in peace, because no matter what, I will never marry your daughter. Am I being clear?"

"And what will I get if I listen?" she asked.

Drew glared at her like she was the most disgusting person on the planet. "If it's money you want, you're not going to get any from me or my family," he said. "But if you stop these attempts on Elizabeth's life, you will get my silence. We will never speak of this again, and you will not face the legal system for attempted murder. Do we have an agreement?"

"What of my family?" she asked. "What are we to do?"

"To be honest, that's not my problem," Drew said. "Although I do consider Lady Catherine a friend, so I will introduce her to friends of mine in London next Season. But you should remember that I am doing that for her, and not for you. Now, I'm only going to ask one more time. Do you agree with my terms?"

"You promise to help find an acceptable match for Catherine?" Lady Givens asked.

"If doing so ensures that you stop these ridiculous attempts on Elizabeth's life, then yes, you have my word," Drew promised.

"Thank you," Lady Givens said helplessly, apparently seeing that she had no other options. "I agree."

With those words, white light filled my vision, and I was on another roller coaster through time. Everything around me went silent. It felt like I was falling forever and would never stop. I think I screamed, but I wouldn't know, since I couldn't hear a thing.

The next thing I knew I was sitting around the table at Misty's shop, my thumb pressed gently against the garnet ring.

CHAPTER 35

"What happened?" Misty asked. "Did it not work? I wouldn't worry about it not working the first time. Things like this take practice. We can keep trying until we get it right."

"No." I blinked away dizziness as my mind adjusted to my surroundings. Drew and Chelsea sat on both sides of me, similarly dazed. "It worked."

Misty looked at me in shock. "But it's only been five seconds! At the least! Yes, I suppose the three of you looked out of it for those five seconds, but ..." She sat back and shook her head, as if she were taking in the magnanimity of what I'd said. "Tell me everything."

Drew, Chelsea, and I spent the next two hours explaining everything that had occurred in our journey to the past. The story got the most interesting when we reached the end. Chelsea hadn't witnessed what had happened with Lady Givens, and while Lady Givens wasn't her real mother—she was Catherine's mother—Chelsea was visibly upset that she had been responsible for attempting to murder my past self.

"I guess once we convinced Lady Givens to stop trying to kill my past self, our mission to the past ended and we returned to the present," I concluded.

"That seems likely," Misty agreed.

"It's crazy that only five seconds passed here." I yawned and rubbed my eyes. Jet lag had nothing on time travel. "We were gone for a week."

"How do we know that it worked?" Drew asked Misty.

"It clearly worked." She laughed. "You just told me the story yourselves!"

"Not the time traveling," he said. "Breaking Chelsea's spell."

"I think it worked," I said before Misty could say anything. "That dark feeling I felt hovering over me before ... it's gone."

Drew looked at me, his eyes intense. "Are you sure?"

"Yes." I nodded. "I'm sure."

"Good." Chelsea breathed a sigh of relief. "I promise I'll never do anything like that again. You believe me that I didn't know what I was doing, right?"

"I believe you," I said, because it was true.

"I can't believe it worked," Misty said, her voice full of amazement. "The three of you know you can never tell anyone about this, right? No one will ever believe you, and they might think you're delusional or in need of serious help. You'll have to keep everything that happened secret for the rest of your lives."

"I don't mind." I found Drew's hand under the table and held it, loving the stability his touch gave me. "The only people I would want to share it with are here with me right now."

"Agreed," Drew said.

The three of us looked at Chelsea.

"Come on." She laughed. "Do you really think I would tell people that I got temporary powers from a witch by drinking her blood, and then used those powers to help my best friend and ex-boyfriend travel back in time so they could stop her past self from being murdered by the mother of my past self?"

I looked at her and raised an eyebrow.

Chelsea opened her mouth in shock. "I'm not *that* crazy!"

"I know," I said. "I was just kidding."

"All right." She stretched her arms in the air. "So, what's next?"

Drew plucked the ring from its place in the center of the table. "I believe this belongs to you," he said, presenting it to me.

I allowed him to slide it onto my finger. It fit perfectly.

"Always and forever," I said once it was securely in place.

This time, we would get our fairy tale ending.

EPILOGUE

Last week I graduated high school, and now I was standing inside the church, ready for the wedding.

Arrangements of white roses adorned the end of each pew, sheer sheets draped between them. The altar was even more incredible—clusters of flowers everywhere, with summer vines winding around the awning over my head. The priest stood with the Bible in hand, ready to begin.

When the wedding march came on, tears formed in my eyes as I watched my mom walk down the aisle. Her dress looked perfect on her—beaded and intricate—and she was radiating happiness.

I was thrilled to be the maid of honor for my mom's marriage to Mr. Givens, and happier to be up there with Chelsea, my future stepsister, who was a bridesmaid.

Drew sat in the front, watching me with love in his eyes. One day, it would be me in my mom's place, walking down the aisle to promise Drew forever. But while we considered ourselves secretly engaged—I never removed the garnet ring—marriage after high school wasn't something either of our families would consider. We knew better than to bring it up to them. Plus, we still had to go to college. We would both be starting Rollins College, a small school in central Florida, in the fall. Chelsea would be at the University of Miami, and while it would be a bit of a drive, we promised we would visit each other whenever possible.

As much as I loved him, waiting to marry Drew was the right decision. We were only eighteen years old. Neither of us minded waiting the four years until finishing our degrees to make our promises to each other official. They were already official to us, and that was what mattered. We had our whole lives ahead of us. There was no need to rush things.

The love between us was strong enough to transcend time—it would last always and forever.

* * *

Did you enjoy this series? Make sure to leave a review for it on Amazon! And read on for a sneak peak of the first book of Michelle's newest series, *Elementals: The Prophecy of Shadows*.

ELEMENTALS

THE PROPHECY OF SHADOWS

Filled with magic, thrilling adventure, and sweet romance, Elementals is the first in a new series that fans of Percy Jackson and The Secret Circle will love!

CHAPTER ONE

The secretary fumbled through the stacks of papers on her desk, searching for my schedule. "Here it is." She pulled out a piece of paper and handed it to me. "I'm Mrs. Dopkin. Feel free to come to me if you have any questions."

"Thanks." I looked at the schedule, which had my name on the top, and listed my classes and their locations. "This can't be right." I held it closer, as if that would make it change. "It has me in all honors classes."

She frowned and clicked around her computer. "Your schedule is correct," she said. "Your homeroom teacher specifically requested that you be in the honors courses."

"But I wasn't in honors at my old school."

"It doesn't appear to be a mistake," she said. "And the late bell's about to ring, so if you need a schedule adjustment, come back at the end of the day so we can discuss it. You're in Mr. Faulkner's homeroom, in the library. Turn right out of the office and walk down the hall. You'll see the library on the right. Go inside and head all the way to the back. Your homeroom is in the only door there. Be sure to hurry—you don't want to be late."

She returned to her computer, apparently done talking to me, so I thanked her for her help and left the office.

Kinsley High felt cold compared to my school in Georgia, and not just in the literal sense. Boxy tan lockers lined every wall, and the concrete floor was a strange mix of browns that reminded me of throw-up. The worst part was that there were no windows anywhere, and therefore a serious lack of sunlight.

I preferred the warm green carpets and open halls at my old school. Actually I preferred everything about my small Georgia town, especially the sprawling house and the peach tree farm I left behind. But I tried not to complain too much to my parents.

After all, I remembered the way my dad had bounced around the living room while telling us about his promotion to anchorman on the news station. It was his dream job, and he didn't mind that the only position available was in Massachusetts. My mom had jumped on board with the plan to move, confident that her paintings would sell better in a town closer to a major city. My younger sister Becca had liked the idea of starting fresh, along with how the shopping in Boston apparently exceeded anything in our town in Georgia.

There had to be something about the move for me to like. Unfortunately, I had yet to find it.

I didn't realize I'd arrived at the library until the double doors were in front of me. At least I'd found it without getting lost.

I walked inside the library, pleased to find it was nothing like the rest of the school. The golden carpet and wooden walls were warm and welcoming, and the upstairs even had windows. I yearned to run toward the sunlight, but the late bell had already rung, so I headed to the back of the library. Hopefully being new would give me a free pass on being late.

Just as the secretary had said, there was only one door. But with it's ancient peeling wood, it looked like it led to a storage room, not a classroom. And there was no glass panel, so I couldn't peek inside. I had to assume this was it.

I wrapped my fingers around the doorknob, my hand trembling. *It's your first day*, I reminded myself. *No one's going to blame you for being late on your first day.*

I opened the door, halfway expecting it to be a closet full of old books or brooms. But it wasn't a closet.

It was a classroom.

Everyone stared at me, and I looked to the front of the room, where a tall, lanky man in a tweed suit stood next to a blackboard covered with the morning announcements. His gray hair shined under the light, and his wrinkled skin and warm smile reminded me more of a grandfather than a teacher.

He cleared his throat and rolled a piece of chalk in his palm. "You must be Nicole Cassidy," he said.

"Yeah." I nodded and looked around at the other students. There were about thirty of them, and there seemed to be an invisible line going down the middle of the room, dividing them in half. The students near the door wore jeans and sweatshirts, but the ones closer to the wall looked like they were dressed for a fashion show instead of school.

"It's nice to meet you Nicole." The teacher sounded sincere, like he was meeting a new friend instead of a student. "Welcome to our homeroom. I'm Mr. Faulkner, but please call me Darius." He turned to the chalkboard, lifted his hand, and waved it from one side to the other. "You probably weren't expecting everything to look so normal, but we have to be careful. As I'm sure you know, we can't risk letting anyone else know what goes on in here."

Then the board shimmered—like sunlight glimmering off the ocean—and the morning announcements changed into different letters right in front of my eyes.

CHAPTER TWO

I blinked a few times to make sure I wasn't hallucinating. What I'd just seen couldn't have been real.

At least the board had stopped shimmering, although instead of the morning announcements, it was full of information about the meanings of different colors. I glanced at the other students, and while a few of them smiled, they were mostly unfazed. They just watched me, waiting for me to say something. Darius also stood calmly, waiting for my reaction.

"How did you do that?" I finally asked.

"It's easy," Darius said. "I used magic. Well, a task like that wouldn't have been easy for you, since you're only in your second year of studies, but given enough practice you'll get the hang of it." He motioned to a seat in the second row, next to a girl with chin-length mousy brown hair. "Please sit down, and we'll resume class."

I stared at him, not moving. "You used ... magic," I repeated, the word getting stuck in my throat. I looked around the room again, waiting for someone to laugh. This had to be a joke. After all, an owl hadn't dropped a letter down my fireplace to let me know I'd been accepted into a special school, and I certainly hadn't taken an enchanted train to get to Kinsley High. "Funny. Now tell me what you *really* did."

"You mean you don't know?" Darius's forehead crinkled.

"Is this a special studies homeroom?" I asked. "And I somehow got put into one about ... magic tricks?"

"It wasn't a trick," said an athletic boy in the center of the room. His sandy hair fell below his ears, and he leaned back in his seat, pushing his sleeves up to his elbows. "Why use tricks when we can do the real thing?"

I stared at him blankly and backed towards the door. He couldn't be serious. Because magic—*real* magic— didn't exist. They must be playing a joke on me. Make fun of the new kid who hadn't grown up in a town so close to Salem.

I wouldn't fall for it. So I might as well play along.

"If that was magic, then where are your wands?" I held up a pretend wand, making a swooshing motion with my wrist.

Darius cleaned his glasses with the bottom of his sweater. "I'd assumed you'd already started your lessons at your previous school." He frowned and placed his glasses back on. "From your reaction, I'm guessing that's not the case. I apologize for startling you. Unfortunately, there's no easy way to say this now, so I might as well be out with it." He took a deep breath, and said, "We're witches. You are, too. And regarding your question, we don't use wands because real witches don't need them. That's an urban legend created by humans who felt safer believing that they couldn't be harmed if there was no wand in sight."

"You can't be serious." I laughed nervously and pulled at the sleeves of my sweater. "Even if witches did exist—which they don't—I'm definitely not one of them."

The only thing "magical" that had ever happened to me was how the ligament I tore in my knee while playing tennis last month had healed right after moving here. The doctor had said it was a medical miracle.

But that didn't make it *magic*.

"I am completely serious," Darius said. "We're all witches, as are you. And this *is* a special studies homeroom—it's for the witches in the school. Although of course the administration doesn't know that." He chuckled. "They just think it's for highly gifted students. Now, please take a seat in the chair next to Kate, and I'll explain more."

I looked around the room, waiting for someone to end this joke. But the brown-haired girl who I assumed was Kate tucked her hair behind her ears and studied her hands. The athletic boy next to her watched me expectantly, and smiled when he caught me looking at him. A girl behind him glanced through her notes, and several other students shuffled in their seats.

My sweater felt suddenly constricting, and I swallowed away the urge to bolt out of there. This was a mistake, and I had to fix it. Now.

"I'm going to go back to the office to make sure they gave me the right schedule," I said, pointing my thumb at the door. "They must have put me in the wrong homeroom. But have fun talking about..." I looked at the board again to remind myself what it said. "Energy colors and their meanings."

They were completely out of their minds.

I hurried out of the classroom, feeling like I could breathe again once I was in the library lobby. No one else was around, and I sat in a chair to collect my thoughts. I would go back to the front office in a minute. For now, I browsed through my cell phone, wanting to see something familiar to remind myself that I wasn't going crazy.

Looking through my friends recent photos made me miss home even more. My eyes filled with tears at the thought of them living their lives without me. It hadn't been a week, and they'd already stopped texting me as often as usual. I was hundreds of miles away, and they were moving on, forgetting about me.

Not wanting anyone to see me crying, I wiped away the tears and switched my camera to front facing view to check my reflection. My eyes were slightly red, but not enough that anyone would notice. And my makeup was still intact.

I was about to put my phone away when I noticed something strange. The small scar above my left eyebrow—the one I'd gotten in fourth grade when I'd fallen on a playground—had disappeared. I brushed my index finger against the place where the indentation had been, expecting it to be a trick of the light. But the skin was soft and smooth.

As if the scar had never been there at all.

I dropped my hand down to my lap. Scars didn't disappear overnight, just like torn ligaments didn't repair themselves in days. And Darius had sounded so convinced that what he'd been saying was true. All of the students seemed to support what he was saying, too.

What if they actually believed what he was telling me? That magic *did* exist?

The thought was entertaining, but impossible. So I clicked out of the camera, put the phone back in my bag, and stood up. I had to get out of here. Maybe once I did, I would start thinking straight again.

"Nicole!" someone called from behind me. "Hold on a second."

I let out a long breath and turned around. The brown-haired girl Darius had called Kate was jogging in my direction. She was shorter than I'd originally thought, and the splattering of freckles across her nose made her look the same age as my younger sister Becca, who was in eighth grade. But that was where the similarities between Kate and Becca ended. Because Kate was relatively plain looking, except for her eyes, which were a unique shade of bright, forest green.

"I know that sounded crazy in there," she said once she reached me. She picked at the side of her thumbnail, and while I suspected she wanted me to tell her that it didn't sound crazy, I couldn't lie like that.

"Yeah. It did." I shifted my feet, gripping the strap of my bag. "I know this is Massachusetts and witches are a part of the history here, so if you all believe in that stuff, that's fine. But it's not really my sort of thing."

"Keep your voice down." She scanned the area, but there was no one else in the library, so we were in the clear. "What Darius told you is real. How else would you explain what you saw in there, when he changed what was on the board?"

"A projector?" I shrugged. "Or maybe the board is a TV screen?"

"There's no projector." She held my gaze. "And the board isn't a television screen, even though that would be cool."

"Then I don't know." I glanced at the doors. "But magic wouldn't be on my list of explanations. No offense or anything."

"None taken," she said in complete seriousness. "But you were put in our homeroom for a reason. You're one of us. Think about it ... do strange things ever happen to you or people around you? Things that have no logical explanation?"

I opened my mouth, ready to say no, but closed it. After all, two miraculous healings in a few days definitely counted as strange, although I wouldn't go so far as to call it *magic*.

But wasn't that the definition of a miracle—something that happened without any logical explanation, caused by something bigger than us? Something *magical*?

"It has." Kate smiled, bouncing on her toes. "Hasn't it?"

"I don't know." I shrugged, not wanting to tell her the specifics. It sounded crazy enough in my head—how would it sound when spoken out loud? "But I guess I'll go back with you for now. Only because the secretary said she won't adjust my schedule until the end of the day, anyway."

She smiled and led the way back to the classroom. Everyone stared at me again when we entered, and I didn't meet anyone's eyes as I took the empty chair next to her.

Darius nodded at us and waited for everyone to settle down. Once situated, I finally glanced around at the other students. The boy Darius had called Chris smiled at me, a girl with platinum hair filed her nails under the table, and the girl next to her looked like she was about to fall asleep. They were all typical high school students waiting for class to end.

But my eyes stopped at the end of the row on a guy with dark shaggy hair. His designer jeans and black leather jacket made him look like he'd come straight from a modeling shoot, and the casual way he leaned back in his chair exuded confidence and a carefree attitude. Then his gaze met mine, and goosebumps rose over my skin. His eyes were a startling shade of burnt brown, and they were soft, but calculating. Like he was trying to figure me out.

Kate rested an elbow on the table and leaned closer to me. "Don't even think about it," she whispered, and I yanked my gaze away from his, my cheeks flushing at the realization that I'd been caught staring at him. "That's Blake Carter. He's been dating Danielle Emerson since last year. She's the one to his left."

Not wanting to stare again, I glanced at Danielle from the corner of my eye. Her chestnut hair was supermodel thick, her ocean blue eyes were so bright that I wondered if they were colored contacts, and her black v-neck shirt dropped as low as possible without being overly inappropriate for school.

Of course Blake had a girlfriend, and she was beautiful. I never stood a chance.

"As I said earlier, we're going to review the energy colors and what they mean," Darius said, interrupting my thoughts. "But before we begin, who can explain to Nicole how we use energy?"

I sunk down in my seat, hating that the attention had been brought back to me. Luckily, the athletic boy next to Kate who'd said the thing earlier about magic not being a trick raised his hand.

"Chris," Darius called on him. "Go ahead."

Chris pushed his hair off his forehead and faced me. His t-shirt featured an angry storm cloud holding a lighting bolt like a baseball bat, with "Trenton Thunder" written below it. It was goofy, and not a sports team that I'd ever heard of. But his boyish grin and rounded cheeks made him attractive in a cute way. Not in the same "stop what you're doing because I'm walking in your direction" way as Blake, but he definitely would have gotten attention from the girls at my old school.

"There's energy everywhere." Chris moved his hands in a giant arc above his head to demonstrate. "Humans know that energy exists—they've harnessed it for electronics. The difference between us and humans is that we have the power to tap into energy and use it ourselves, and humans don't." He smiled at me, as if I was supposed to understand what he meant. "Make sense?"

"Not really," I said. "Sorry."

"It's easier if you relate it to something familiar," he said, speaking faster. "What happens to the handle of a metal spoon when you leave it in boiling water?"

"It gets hot?" I said it as a question. This was stuff people learned in fifth grade science—not high school homeroom.

"And what happens when it's plastic?"

"It doesn't get hot," I said slowly. "It stays room temperature."

"Exactly." He grinned at me like I'd just solved an astrophysics mathematical equation. "Humans are like plastic. Even if they're immersed in energy, they can't conduct it. Witches are like metal. We have the ability to absorb energy and control it as we want."

"So, how do we take in this energy?" I asked, since I might as well humor him.

"Through our hands." Chris turned his palms up, closed his eyes, and took a deep breath. He looked like a meditating Buddha. Students snickered, and Chris re-opened his eyes, pushed his sleeves up, and sat back in his chair.

"O-o-kay." I elongated the word, smiling and laughing along with everyone else.

Darius cleared his throat, and everyone calmed down. "We can conduct energy from the Universe into our bodies," he said, his voice full of authority. Chills passed through me, and even though I still didn't believe any of this, I sat back to listen. "Once we've harnessed it, we can use it as we like. Think of energy like light. It contains different colors, each relating to an aspect of life. I've written them on the board. The most basic exercise we learn in this class is to sense this energy and absorb it. Just open your mind, envision the color you're focusing on, and picture it entering your body through your palms."

I rotated my hand to look at my palm. It looked normal—not like it was about to open up and absorb energy from the Universe.

"We're going to do a meditation session," Darius continued. "Everyone should pick a color from the board and picture it as energy entering your palms. Keep it simple and absorb the energy—don't push it back out into the Universe. This exercise is for practice and self-improvement." He looked at me, a hint of challenge in his eyes. "Now, please pick a color and begin."

I looked around the room to see what others were doing. Most people already had their eyes closed, the muscles in their faces calm and relaxed. They were really getting into this. As if they truly believed it.

If I didn't at least *look* like I was trying, I would stand out—again. So I might as well go along with it and pretend.

I re-examined the board and skimmed through the "meanings" of the colors. Red caught my attention first.

It apparently increased confidence, courage, and love, along with attraction and desire. The prospect made me glance at Blake, who sat still with his eyes closed, his lips set in a line of concentration.

But he was out of my league *and* he had a girlfriend. I shouldn't waste my time hoping for anything to happen between us.

Instead, I read through the other colors and settled on green. It supposedly brought growth, success, and luck, along with helping a person open their mind, become more aware of options, and choose a good path. Those were all things I needed right now.

I opened my palms towards the ceiling and closed my eyes. Once comfortable, I steadied my breathing and tried clearing my mind.

Then there was the question of how to "channel" a color. Picturing it seemed like a good start, so I imagined myself pulling green out of the air, the color glowing with life. A soft hum filled my ears as it expanded and pushed against me, like waves crashing over my skin. The palms of my hands tingled, and the energy flowed through my body, joining with my blood as it pumped through my veins. It streamed up my arms, moved down to my stomach, and poured down to my toes. Green glowed behind my eyelids, and I kept gathering it and gathering it until it grew so much that it had nowhere else to go.

Then it pushed its way out of my palms with such force that it must have lit up the entire room.

ABOUT THE AUTHOR

Michelle Madow grew up in Baltimore, graduated Rollins College in Orlando, and now lives in Boca Raton, Florida. She wrote her first book in her junior year of college, and has been writing novels since. Some of her favorite things are: reading, pizza, traveling, shopping, time travel, Broadway musicals, and spending time with friends and family. Michelle has toured across America to promote her books and to encourage high school students to embrace reading and writing. Someday, she hopes to travel the world for a year on a cruise ship.

Follow her on:
Facebook:/MichelleMadow
Twitter/Instagram: @MichelleMadow
Snapchat: MichLMadow

Visit Michelle online at www.michellemadow.com.

To get exclusive content and instant updates on Michelle's new books, visit her website and subscribe to her newsletter!

44908170R10153

Made in the USA
San Bernardino, CA
27 January 2017